"Are you looking forward to work tomorrow?"

"I am, actually. Working, having a *gut* job, earning an income—those are things not to be taken for granted."

When he didn't explain any further, Sarah said, "You're a bit mysterious. You know that. Right?"

Noah shrugged. "There's no use explaining what others can't possibly understand."

"How do you know until you try?"

His voice dropped, and he said, "I know."

He sat forward, elbows propped on his legs, fingers interlaced, studying his hands for a moment. "People think they want their questions answered, but they don't. They basically feel left out when they don't know something, even if that something is none of their business."

Sarah felt the first stirrings of irritation. "Maybe they simply want to help."

"Maybe. Or it could be they're bored with their own lives."

"That's a bit unkind." Even as she said it, she thought of the conversation she'd overheard. Did those two women want to help Noah? Or were they just bored with their own lives?

"I didn't mean it that way." He stood and stretched. "I should be getting back."

Vannetta Chapman has published over one hundred articles in Christian family magazines and received over two dozen awards from Romance Writers of America chapter groups. She discovered her love for the Amish while researching her grandfather's birthplace of Albion, Pennsylvania. Her first novel, *A Simple Amish Christmas*, quickly became a bestseller. Chapman lives in Texas Hill Country with her husband.

Books by Vannetta Chapman

Love Inspired

Indiana Amish Market

An Amish Proposal for Christmas
Her Amish Adversary
An Unusual Amish Winter Match
The Mysterious Amish Bachelor

Indiana Amish Brides

A Widow's Hope
Amish Christmas Memories
A Perfect Amish Match
The Amish Christmas Matchmaker
An Unlikely Amish Match
The Amish Christmas Secret
An Amish Winter
"Stranded in the Snow"
The Baby Next Door
An Amish Baby for Christmas
The Amish Twins Next Door

Visit the Author Profile page at LoveInspired.com for more titles.

The Mysterious Amish Bachelor

VANNETTA CHAPMAN

PLEASE RECYCLE · THIS PRODUCT IS RECYCLABLE

Recycling programs for this product may not exist in your area.

ISBN-13: 978-1-335-59876-9

The Mysterious Amish Bachelor

For questions and comments about the quality of this book, please contact us at CustomerService@Harlequin.com.

® is a trademark of Harlequin Enterprises ULC.

Love Inspired
22 Adelaide St. West, 41st Floor
Toronto, Ontario M5H 4E3, Canada
www.LoveInspired.com

Printed in U.S.A.

Love one another.
—*John* 13:34

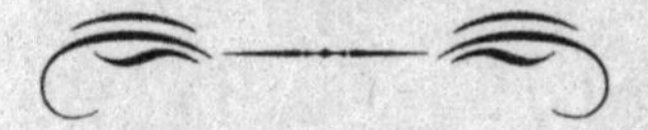

This book is dedicated to my grandmother

Chapter One

May 1
Shipshewana, Indiana

Sarah Yoder moved the chicken casserole to the side on the oven rack, slipped the pan of biscuits in beside it, shut the oven door and turned to stare out the kitchen window.

"He's here," Eunice groaned.

"It won't be so bad."

"Oh, you think so? Last week *Dat* insisted that I take some important papers over to Jesse Hochstetler."

"Uh-oh."

"Yeah. He's tried to match each of us with that poor man."

Sarah gave Eunice a quick hug. "When you're as old as I am, he stops trying."

"I don't know if that makes me feel better or worse."

"Exactly."

They both turned to peer out the window at

Noah Beiler. He was average height, average build, average Amish. Sarah realized that was an uncharitable thought. He was, no doubt, a perfectly nice guy.

Eunice sighed as if the evening were a heavy shawl lying across her shoulders. "Didn't you go to school with him?"

"I did, but that was a long time ago."

"Looks like they're going to sit on the porch for a spell."

"Mind taking out two glasses of tea?"

Eunice rolled her eyes, but she reached for the glasses Sarah had prepared. The ice was from the trays they kept in the freezer. It wasn't as if they had an ice maker. They were Amish. They believed in living Plain. No electricity. No automobiles. No wireless internet.

The tea had been brewed in the sun.

"Might as well get this over with. Do I have any grease on my face?"

"Nope. You look remarkably grease-free at the moment."

Which caused them both to laugh. Eunice did usually have dirt or oil or grease on her face. She was a tinkerer. She was happiest when working in the barn or the pastures or even the garden, and Sarah loved her dearly for it.

They were an especially close family, maybe because their *mamm* had died when her youngest sister, Ada, was only a babe. As the oldest,

Sarah had helped to guide her four *schweschdern* through childhood, teen years and into young adulthood.

One of them was usually dating, but never anything serious. It seemed—even to Sarah—as if they were content to live at home, to be with their family.

Just when it looked as if their *dat* would grow old at home with all of his *doschdern* unmarried, three of their *schweschdern* had married in the last few years. They'd also added two *bopplin* to the family, both born before Christmas the year before. It was hard to believe her nieces were now seventeen months old and walking!

There were days when Sarah thought she couldn't imagine being happier than she was now.

Then there were days when loneliness threatened to overwhelm her.

She couldn't explain why her emotions careened from one extreme to the other, but she'd learned to wait it out, to trust in *Gotte*'s plan for her life, to stay focused on the present moment. It wasn't always easy, especially when her *dat* had a matchmaking plan in his back pocket. Sarah could only hope that Noah Beiler was there to meet Eunice because she was personally not feeling up to any dating games.

She heard Eunice speak to their visitor, then tell them dinner would be ready in fifteen minutes.

Eunice walked back into the room, smiling and shaking her head. "I think this one's for you."

"Why would you say that?"

"Because *Dat* didn't spend any time explaining about my inventions. And he was talking up your cooking."

Now it was Sarah's turn to groan.

"You are a pretty *gut* cook."

"I've had lots of experience."

"Anything I can do to help?"

"Toss the salad?"

"Sure thing."

Twenty minutes later, the four of them were seated at the table. They bowed their heads for a silent prayer, Amos gave a hearty, "Amen," and they began passing dishes. Sarah tried to be inconspicuous about studying Noah. He was better looking than she remembered, with a strong jawline and kind eyes. He caught her staring, smiled in an embarrassed way, then passed the salad to Eunice.

"You went to school with Sarah, *ya*?" Amos dug into the chicken casserole with gusto. He'd had some health challenges in recent years, and Sarah was relieved to see his vigorous appetite.

"*Ya*. It's been quite a few years though, right, Sarah?"

"It has. I seem to remember you playing marbles a lot."

Noah laughed and nodded his head. "Something our teacher did not abide very well."

"Could have been worse. Could have been frogs or snakes."

"I must have had a different teacher than you two." Eunice buttered her biscuit, studying it as if she could see the past there. Popping a bite in her mouth, she chewed and then said, "You would never have dared to play marbles or have frogs or snakes with Beth Bender. That woman was serious about education."

"Are your other *doschdern* still in the area, Amos?"

"Oh, *ya*. Indeed, they are. Becca and Gideon live in the new house across from the barn. You passed it as you drove in. They would have joined us but Gideon was working late on some incoming auction items."

"Becca thinks that Mary is teething again," Sarah added. "Their *boppli* is seventeen months old, and she is quite the handful. We adore both her and Lydia, Bethany's child. They were born only hours apart."

"Those were busy times—frightening times if I'm honest. There were problems with both pregnancies." Amos stared across the room as if he could see the entire family gathered in the waiting room of the hospital—worried, scared, praying. Finally, he shook his head and returned to the present moment. "Bethany married Aaron King, who you'll meet sometime this week at the market. As Sarah mentioned, they also have a *boppli*, named Lydia. Then Ada surprised us all by marrying Aaron's *bruder*, Ethan."

"Your family is going through a busy time." Noah's voice was soft, gentle even, as if he appreciated all that those three marriages and two pregnancies entailed.

"What about your family, Noah?" Sarah told herself she wasn't being nosy. She was genuinely interested. It seemed that Noah had dropped off the radar quite a few years ago. Had it been five years? More? He had moved out of the area and left his parents to run the farm alone. It was all coming back to her now. No one ever said where he'd gone or why.

"My parents are *gut*. *Dat*'s still running things on the farm and only needs help for planting and harvesting. Which is why I have the time to work at the market."

"Definitely a blessing for me," Amos added. "There are a lot of things I hope to get done over the next few months."

It amazed Sarah how much was involved with running the Shipshewana Outdoor Market—the largest market in the Midwest. The largest Amish owned and operated market in Indiana. Her *dat* had first worked as an auctioneer, then risen to assistant manager, general manager and finally owner. He definitely needed a lot of help to keep the market running according to his standards.

He was careful about whom he hired—always looking for the most qualified and dependable person. On the other hand, he would occasionally hire someone who was down on their luck.

So which was Noah?

An answer to one of her *dat*'s prayers?

Or someone that he was trying to offer a helping hand?

And if it was the second of those, why did Noah Beiler, a seemingly able-bodied man, need her *dat*'s help?

Sarah was surprised that Noah was still there when she and Eunice had finished cleaning the kitchen.

"I'm going to the barn," Eunice whispered.

"Don't leave me here alone with them. It's… awkward."

"Sorry, sis. But my being in the room won't help that one bit."

She ducked out the back door, shutting it silently behind her. At that moment, Sarah would have been happy to go to the barn and work on a solar pump or a cranky old generator. She wasn't mechanically minded like Eunice, but she could hand her a tool or brush a horse.

Still, as the woman of the house, her responsibilities lay in the sitting room. She squared her shoulders, poured coffee into three mugs, placed applesauce cookies on a plate, added three napkins, a crock of sugar and a small pitcher of milk, and picked up the tray. Perhaps Noah would eat so many cookies he'd become sleepy and decide to go home.

He didn't.

He ate one cookie, and he seemed content to stay and visit with her *dat*.

"You mentioned renovation projects, but you weren't specific. What did you have in mind?"

"The bathrooms need updating. New paint. New tile. New fixtures."

"Easy enough."

"I'd also like you to look at the canteen. It's a favorite among tourists and employees alike, but even I can see that it needs a fresh look."

"I'm happy to do that."

"There are other projects that I've been putting off…certainly enough to keep you busy through the summer. We'll also assign a few part-timers to your work crew."

"Sounds great, Amos. *Danki*."

"Don't thank me. You'll be the one doing the work."

Sarah figured she might as well ply Noah for information if she was going to spend her evening hearing about projects at the market. "So you have experience in construction?"

"Not construction as much as remodeling."

"There's a difference?"

"*Ya*. For sure and certain there is."

When he didn't elaborate, she tried again. "What kind of jobs have you done before?"

He met her gaze, didn't blink or look uncomfortable in any way. "This and that."

"I checked his references, Sarah. No need to worry." Amos laughed heartily.

Sarah simply smiled. It had been obvious to her that Noah was quite vague with his answers. What was that about? Perhaps she should be less circumspect. Get off the subject of work and ask more general questions. "Where did you live the years you were gone?"

"Here and there."

"Do those places have a name?"

"Illinois—mainly."

"Ah."

So not so far away. Then why hadn't he been home? At least she couldn't remember him coming to visit his parents. Theirs was a large church community, so it was possible that he had and she hadn't noticed.

Amos told a few stories about the market. He described Ada becoming an Amish animal activist, then falling in love with Ethan. He explained about Bethany and Aaron working together in the RV park that was adjacent to the market. "They fell *in lieb* as well."

At this point, Noah was staring at his feet, and Sarah wanted to melt into the rocking chair.

"Then there was Becca and Gideon. He'll tell you their story, but suffice to say it was firecrackers before it was love."

Noah nodded as if that made sense.

"You never know what might happen when you come to work at the market. You, too, could find yourself marrying before the year's out."

"Oh, I don't expect that's in my immediate future." Noah popped up off the couch, clearly uncomfortable with the direction the conversation had taken. "Thank you for having me over, Amos. I look forward to working with you."

Sarah and Amos stood as well.

"And thank you, Sarah, for the fine meal."

"We're happy you could join us."

"You're welcome any time," Amos added. "We usually have a busy, bustling house. It isn't often that you'll have an evening here this quiet. Perhaps you could eat with us the next off-Sunday. And bring your parents, of course."

"*Danki*. I'll pass the invitation along to them."

"I have some reading to do before bed. Sarah, would you mind seeing Noah out?"

See him out? The door was eight feet from the couch.

"I'd be happy to."

They walked out onto the porch together, the screen door slapping shut behind them. Sarah heard her *dat* whistling as he made his way to his room. The sun had set but a soft light lingered, and she could make out their horses in the pasture. The crops in the field. Becca's house with lantern light shining from her *boppli*'s room.

Eunice remained in the barn, tinkering, no doubt having forgotten all about them.

Their farm, though it wasn't large, was home.

It was all Sarah had ever known.

She couldn't imagine living somewhere else. She couldn't begin to fathom anything that would require her to leave for years and not at least return for a visit. She certainly couldn't think of a single valid reason for Noah's prolonged absence.

What kind of person did that to their parents?

What kind of son ignored the needs of his family?

Not that it was any of her business. She was a naturally inquisitive person, but she tried to curb that tendency.

The evening had been embarrassing, and the man standing beside her had done nothing to deserve being put on the spot. Never one to let a thing go unsaid, she turned to Noah to offer an apology for her *dat*'s obvious attempt to set them up.

Noah started speaking at the same time as Sarah.

"You go ahead," she said.

"*Nein*. You. I didn't mean to…interrupt."

They had walked to his buggy, or rather, his

parents' buggy. The horse seemed content, cropping at the new grass that was close enough to reach. It was a chestnut mare, and Sarah put her hand on its neck. It seemed to Noah that she was avoiding looking at him, but then he could have been imagining that. When you spent five years locked in a concrete block with thousands of other men, you learned to watch every visual tick, every small change in another person's expression.

"I wanted to apologize for my *dat*'s behavior."

"Amos?" Noah removed his hat and ran a hand through his hair, which was too long. Why hadn't he taken the time to have it cut? He'd be examined closely enough without trying to bring attention to himself. "Amos is a *gut* guy. I appreciate him hiring me."

"Why did he hire you?" She turned and looked at him squarely now.

"Because I needed a job, and I suppose…" He wasn't offended by her question, but he also had the feeling that it was best to quell her curiosity now. Of course, he couldn't tell her everything. "I suppose because my references were *gut*."

"You've been gone…how long?"

"Since I was twenty-one."

"And you're my age."

"I'll turn thirty-one this summer."

"Same." She stepped away from the mare after a final affectionate pat.

He'd forgotten so much about home. Maybe because it had been too painful to remember. The way the light played across the fields. The quietness of the farms. The love these people had for their animals. The habit of lingering over dinner and then sitting on the porch or in the living room and enjoying coffee.

"Ten years. That's a long time, Noah."

"It is."

She waited, and he let her wait. There was a time to supply answers, and there was a time to let silence have its way. Wisdom was in knowing the difference. Noah didn't consider himself a wise man, but he had learned a lot in prison. He'd had to. It was learn or become like the men he shared a cell with, and he'd refused to let that happen. That would have been a bigger tragedy than losing eight years of his life.

Sarah Yoder shook her head, then returned to the previous topic, the thing she felt a need to apologize for. "What happened tonight...in my house...was a setup, and I'm sorry."

"Why are you sorry?"

"Because it's embarrassing."

His laugh was full, deep, surprising even to him.

So, he hadn't forgotten how to laugh, to let his worries go, to enjoy a moment as dusk settled across the land, standing next to a beautiful woman. And Sarah Yoder was a beautiful woman. He wondered why she hadn't married, though he seemed to remember that she almost did once. It was too long ago to dredge up the details, and did they really matter? *Nein*. Past was past and best left alone.

"It's our parents' way, Sarah. It's what they know. Probably what was done for them. We're way beyond marrying age, in case you haven't noticed."

"Oh, I've noticed."

"I'm sure we each have our own reasons."

She didn't answer, merely nodded.

"But your *dat* cares about you very much. Not that I'm such a *gut* catch." He leaned forward and lowered his voice in a conspiratorial whisper. "There are those missing years to account for."

He thought she might laugh.

He hoped she would.

Instead, she wagged a finger at him. "You talk a good game, Noah Beiler, but you also avoid answering questions."

He shrugged.

Best not to deny what she'd already figured out.

"Again, *danki* for dinner. It was delicious, and the company was charming." He climbed up into the buggy, released the brake and called out to Ginger.

He started laughing once he was out on the county road, and wasn't that a thing of wonder that he could find amusement in an awkward situation. He hadn't been sure what Amos's intentions were in inviting him to dinner, but the old guy had definitely been trying to set him up with his daughter, Sarah. He'd been quite obvious about it too, which was part of what Noah found so amusing.

One thing he knew for certain was that Sarah Yoder was way out of his league. If she knew his history, she wouldn't give him a second glance. Not because she was unkind, but because she was the very image of conventional. The puzzling thing was that Amos *did* know where he'd spent the last eight years, and the two before that as well.

Amos knew everything about him.

Noah had insisted on that when his parents had first suggested he work at the market. It was a condition of his parole, that his employer knew his history. He wouldn't be violating those rules because if there was one thing Noah was absolutely sure of, it was that he would not be going back to the Illinois State Prison. *Nein.* He'd learned whatever lessons were there for him. He'd changed. He had no fear of backsliding.

But coming home?

That had been a chancy thing.

He could expect more probing questions, curious glances, perhaps even a few direct interrogations. It was unusual for an Amish man or woman to leave home, to stay away for a decade, and then to come back. His neighbors and acquaintances and coworkers would be naturally curious. He'd have to sidestep those questions carefully because he could not tell them he'd been a drug user, then arrested and finally incarcerated. The state of Illinois had declared he'd paid his debt, but the Amish community in Shipshewana, Indiana, might not be so quick to forgive.

They would justifiably be concerned.

They'd need time to accept that he was a changed man.

Some would never believe that.

Many people talked a good game about giving second chances, but when it came down to it, that sort of compassion was rare indeed. Best to keep his past in the past.

Even if it meant frustrating pretty Sarah Yoder.

Soon enough, her attention would turn away from him. That's what he truly hoped for. What he prayed for. That people would see him and forget about his missing years. That people would allow him to come home.

Chapter Two

Sarah did not spend the rest of the week thinking about Noah Beiler—at least, not all of it. She did ask her *schweschdern* if they knew anything about his past. Becca cut up a banana and set it on the tray attached to Mary's high chair.

"I barely remember him since he was four years ahead of me in school. You know how the older boys were. They wouldn't give us younger girls a second look."

"It's just that I wonder where he was all those years."

"Ask him."

"I did, or rather I gave him every opportunity to tell me."

"And?"

"He chose not to."

"Well, there you have it." Becca looked out the window, a familiar distant expression on her face. Becca had spent some time away before marrying Gideon. She'd worked with Mennonite Disaster Services. After they were married, Becca and Gideon had even served together on a job-site in Texas.

She'd been deeply affected by her time helping people less fortunate. It was something that had changed her, matured her, caused her to see things differently from the rest of them. Sarah envied her *schweschder*'s ability to show strangers genuine compassion.

When Mary banged her spoon against the high chair tray, Becca focused her attention back on her daughter. Reaching for the cereal box, she placed a handful on the tray, and Mary rewarded them both with a toothy smile.

"Sometimes, people aren't ready to share their past, for a variety of reasons. If you want my opinion, I'd suggest you give him time."

"I guess."

"What choice do you have?"

"Well, I could get all nosy and ask around."

"If you don't know, I doubt anyone else does either. Other than his parents."

"And *Dat*."

"You know he won't share anything personal about an employee."

"True."

"But he must trust the guy, or he wouldn't have tried to set you up with him."

Sarah drummed her fingertips against her lips and stared up at the ceiling. Finally, she said, "I'm too old for this. I can see *Dat* trying to find a husband for Eunice, but not for me."

"Why?"

"Why?"

"Yes. Why not for you? Do you never plan to marry?"

Sarah waved away the question.

"I'm serious." Becca reached across the table and put her hands on top of Sarah's, gave them a warm squeeze. "*Gotte* has a plan for you, same as the rest of us."

"But maybe it doesn't include marriage."

"Fair enough. But maybe it does."

After that, Becca graciously let the conversation drift to more comfortable topics—the family garden, the market, diaper rash.

In the end, Sarah did not ask around about Noah Beiler for two reasons. The first was because she spent most of the week at home. There was no one to ask! The other reason was that even when she did go into town twice on errands, she couldn't bring herself to be nosy. Curiosity was healthy when it didn't hurt anyone, when it didn't cross personal boundaries. Nosiness was something that was rude and disrespectful. It wasn't her way.

But she did turn the topic of Noah's missing years over and over in her mind.

Ten years was a long time to be gone.

Where had he been?

And why was he back now?

Those questions remained unanswered, even when he formally joined their church's congregation on Sunday morning. Most people who were Amish had been raised in the faith. Even considering time for *rumspringa*—a chance to try *Englisch* things—most who joined did so by their early twenties. Sarah had been only nineteen when she'd committed her life to the Lord and to their Plain ways.

The Sunday service was held at Bethany and Aaron's home. It was also Ada and Ethan's home. The two King brothers had been raised on the small farm, and now they were raising their own families there. The house had been expanded, the barn repaired and the little farm on Huckleberry Lane now looked like any other. Crops had been newly planted in the fields. Horses were pastured adjacent to the barn, the area surrounded by solid fencing. The days of poverty and sorrow for the old homestead had passed.

It seemed to Sarah that their entire community was experiencing a time of growth and blessing. The church service took place on the sunny side of the house, the family's vegetable garden growing lushly just past where the benches for their service had been placed.

Now, as she watched Noah walk to the front of those assembled, Sarah felt tears prick her eyes. It never ceased to touch her heart when someone made this commitment. She'd witnessed it dozens of times before, maybe hundreds.

Still, it felt tender and special and holy.

Noah sat on the bench that had been placed at the front, facing the congregation. Bishop Ezekiel held out his hands, cupped together. Gideon, who the year before had been chosen as a deacon, picked up the ladle, dipped it into the bucket and poured water into Ezekiel's hands. The bishop held his hands over Noah's head, allowing the water to cascade over him—once, twice, then a third time.

Noah sat with one hand covering his face, indicating his submission and humility. It was a posture that was gentle, vulnerable. The fact that he was thirty years old and only now committing himself to the Lord made it even more special.

Sarah noticed Noah's mother wiping at her eyes with a handkerchief. How long had she prayed for this moment? How often had her heart broken over her son? How deeply had she missed him?

Bishop Ezekiel didn't attempt to explain Noah's absence from their midst. Instead he thanked *Gotte* that the young man was now home. "As Noah commits his life to the Lord and to this church, each of you are to commit yourself to praying for Noah and his path forward. Pray that he will continue in his walk of humility, that he will grow ever closer to our Lord and that he will find his place within this group and within our community."

Amens came from all the congregants. As Sarah watched, Noah wiped the water from his face, and somehow she knew that tears were mingled with the water. She didn't doubt for a moment that his commitment was sincere and that he would be a valued member of their community and their church.

His past—no matter how mysterious—was no longer relevant.

Thirty minutes later, she was standing in the serving line when he stopped by.

"This is where your *schweschdern* live now?"

She noticed his hair was still damp from the baptism. "*Ya.* It's the old King place, actually. Ethan and Aaron were gifted it from their parents."

"Nice."

"You might not have said that if you'd visited it a few years ago."

"Ya?"

"They've put a lot of work into the buildings and the fields. You should see what they've done to the back pastures and the pond beyond."

"Perhaps you could show it to me later."

Sarah blinked rapidly, dropped the serving spoon into the potato salad, fished it out, and wiped it off with a dish towel. When was the last time a man had asked her to take a walk? Why was Noah asking her now?

"*Ya*. Of course. I'd be happy to."

The next twenty minutes passed in a cloud of confusion. She spooned macaroni salad onto her *dat*'s plate when he asked for coleslaw. Then she bumped into a pitcher of tea and knocked it off the table. When she took her plate to sit with her *schweschdern*, she found that she'd given herself meat with no vegetables. She felt unbalanced and more than a little confused—all over an invitation to take a walk. It was embarrassing! Fortunately, no one else seemed to notice.

They were talking of summer plans, growing families and what a relief the rain was after the dry summer of two years before. She picked at her slice of ham and tried to answer coherently when a remark was addressed to her. Finally, she excused herself and fled into the main house to use the restroom. She studied her reflection in the mirror.

Why were her cheeks so red?

Why did the day feel suddenly hot?

And why-oh-why was she acting like a lovelorn school girl?

She was not interested in a relationship with Noah Beiler.

It was simply that he was the first man to pay her any attention in quite some time. Her embarrassment didn't mean she felt anything for him in a romantic way. It meant that she needed to socialize more.

She was drying her hands when she became aware of a conversation outside the door. Two women were speaking in hushed voices, though she couldn't make out who exactly. She could, however, catch the gist of what they were saying.

"I heard that he followed a girl to California."

"I heard he left the country."

"Either way, he's hiding something."

"Which Ezekiel did not bring up."

"To be fair, he wasn't a member of our congregation when he did whatever he did. It isn't as if he broke any rules. How could he if he wasn't even committed to those rules?"

"And yet no one's *rumspringa* lasts that long."

"His poor parents…"

It took Sarah a moment to realize that whoever had been talking had walked away. She jerked open the bathroom door and hurried down the hall, nearly colliding with Ada.

"You look twirled out of shape. What's wrong?"

"Nothing."

"Are you sure?"

"Nothing we can do anything about." Sarah sighed and looped an arm through her youngest *schweschder*'s. "Now tell me what's happening at your job with the SPCA. I feel like we haven't talked in forever."

They walked out into the May sunshine, chatting and laughing, and Sarah felt marginally better. Then Noah, standing near the dessert table, caught her attention and nodded toward the path that led back to the small pond.

"Did Noah Beiler just wink at you?"

"It wasn't a wink."

"It was something."

"I told him that I'd show him the improvements you all have made."

"In the fields?"

Sarah laughed. "At the back pond."

"My favorite spot. I'd tag along, but I've heard three is a litter." She squeezed Sarah's hand, then headed off in the direction of Ethan.

Sarah didn't realize Noah had joined her until he said, "They look like a sweet couple."

She jumped, shook her head at her silliness, then said, "Another case of opposites attract. Still want to see the pond?"

"Sure. I feel like I'm on display in a shop window the way people keep looking at me."

Sarah laughed.

"What's so funny?"

"Well, you brought it on yourself. Stay away for ten years and people grow curious." She thought of the unkind conversation she'd overheard, but decided it wasn't worth repeating. That was how gossip spread. People repeating what someone else said. She had no desire to be a part of that.

Still, it did concern her that Noah was the subject of the Amish grapevine.

"Why the somber look?" He bumped a shoulder against hers.

"I was just thinking that people are disappointing at times."

"That they are."

Noah Beiler was not the kind of guy who felt like he needed to fill a silence. They walked quietly along the path toward the pond. Somewhere along that path, Sarah's tension melted away. The sun was shining, the temperature was absolutely lovely, and the little farm on Huckleberry Lane was a place of such joy, love and peace that she found herself pulled into its special charm.

She explained how Ada had always been the baby of their family. "We probably did spoil her. She never knew *Mamm*, and I think we tried to make up for that."

"Must have been hard losing your mom when you were…what…a *kinder*, *ya*?"

"I was eleven, actually. Not a child, but certainly not grown."

"Your family seems to have weathered the hard times."

"I suppose." She told him about Becca's desire to travel and how that had dovetailed into working for MDS. She explained about her father's heart problems. She described Ada and Ethan's rough beginning, before they'd even realized they had feelings for each other.

"Ada used to say that she wasn't going to fall head over *kapp* strings with anyone."

"Head over *kapp* strings? Do you mean head over heels?"

"She's always seen things in her own special way."

The field on their left had recently been planted with corn. Tiny shoots of green had already popped up through the rich dirt. To their right Ethan had planted soybean, but it had yet to push through the tilled soil.

As they turned a corner, the small pond lay before them. Noah let out a long, low whistle. "We should have held church services back here."

"It's nice, right?"

Ethan and Aaron had built a gazebo near the water, so that the children could play in the shade. A wooden picnic table sat off to one side, and four rocking chairs were lined up facing the water. Noah sank into one of the chairs with a groan.

"That sounded as if it came from my *dat*."

"*Ya*. I make a lot of old man sounds now."

"You're calling me old? Remember, we are the same age."

He jerked his head toward her, then laughed. "You had me there. I thought I'd offended you."

"Oh, I'm not that easily offended." She added, "*Dat* says that growing old is a blessing."

"My parents say the same, though I'm not looking forward to arthritis and poor eyesight."

"I suppose we have a few years before those things become concerns."

They sat in the chairs, rocking back and forth, laughing when four turtles climbed out onto a log to warm themselves in the sunshine.

"Are you looking forward to work tomorrow?"

"I am, actually. Working, having a *gut* job, earning an income, those are things not to be taken for granted."

When he didn't explain any further, Sarah said, "You're a bit mysterious. You know that, right?"

Noah shrugged. "There's no use explaining what others can't possibly understand."

"How do you know until you try?"

His voice dropped, and he said, "I know."

He sat forward, elbows propped on his legs, fingers interlaced, studying his hands for a moment. "People think they want their questions answered, but they don't. They basically feel left out when they don't know something, even if that something is none of their business."

Sarah felt the first stirrings of irritation. "Maybe they simply want to help."

"Maybe. Or it could be they're bored with their own lives."

"That's a bit unkind." Even as she said it, she thought of the conversation she'd overheard. Did those two women want to help Noah? Or were they just bored with their own lives?

"I didn't mean it that way." He stood and stretched. "I should be getting back. My pop enjoys a nap on Sunday afternoons."

"Another perk of old age."

"I like a good nap too." Noah grinned at her in a challenging way.

"I read…but sometimes it ends in a nap."

As they walked back following the same path they had come, Sarah replayed their conversation in her mind. Noah apparently thought he would be able to handle his past and present alone. But that wasn't their way. It wasn't what being part of a community meant. How could others help him if he insisted on keeping himself isolated? It wouldn't be long before he'd be feeling on the outside of things, and then he'd become lonely and bitter and then he'd move away again.

She thought that would be a real shame.

Surely, there was some woman in their congregation who would make a good match for Noah.

She wasn't interested in him—not romantically speaking.

She could never love someone who was able to leave their family for ten years. Family meant everything to her. She couldn't think of a single valid reason to stay away for that long. She told herself she wasn't judging him. Perhaps there was something lacking in his personality—like devotion or responsibility or a sense of what was right and what was wrong.

Whatever the reason, he was a part of their community now.

As a part of the group who only hours earlier had promised to pray for him, Sarah didn't think she should allow him to struggle with his past alone. In one very real sense, they were their brother's keeper. They were duty-bound to help. And suddenly, she had an idea for just how she might do that.

Noah tried not to think of Sarah as he drove his parents home, fetched the book he'd been reading and sprawled out on his bed. He couldn't keep his mind on the words, though. Finally, he closed the book and went outside, walked the perimeter of their property, let the memories of his childhood flood his soul.

He'd missed this place so much.

Missed his parents.

Even missed the church services—though he had no use for people who gossiped, and yes, he'd heard a few whispering about his "missing years."

He didn't know why he'd asked Sarah to go for a walk. Perhaps it was because she at least asked her questions directly. He laughed, remembering the look of frustration on her face. Sarah Yoder was someone he wouldn't mind knowing better. But there was no use in pursuing that. Though he might be able to keep his past private, keep it out of the local paper and out of circulation in the Amish grapevine, he would never try to keep such a secret from his *fraa*.

Fraa?

She'd taken one walk with him, and he was daydreaming about marriage?

What he needed was work. A good solid eight hours would drive any romantic notions from his mind. He could probably blame such thoughts on all of the young couples, babies and children. An Amish church service invariably had more little ones than adults, since most families had eight to ten children.

That was possible for other people.

Probably it was even possible for Sarah Yoder.

What it wasn't, though, was possible for him.

He survived the idle hours of Sunday, managed to sleep a good seven hours and rose early for his new job the next day.

He spent Monday calculating estimates for the work in the bathrooms and the canteen. When he turned the numbers in to Amos, he learned that he'd meet his part-time crew the next day.

"Gideon has already ordered a few of these supplies," Amos said, ticking off items on his list. "I'll pass this on to him. Everything else you need should be in by the end of the week. In the meantime, you can at least get started on the demolition portion of the bathroom job."

Noah whistled all the way home, cared for the horse, then made his way into his parents' house. Very little had changed since he was a *youngie*. The home was small because his *mamm* had not been able to have additional children after he was born. Perhaps he'd felt the weight of their hopes and dreams as a young man. Being an only child was rare indeed in an Amish community.

Though small, the house had been well cared for. His room was on the side of the house with the kitchen. His parents' room was on the opposite side, adjacent to the sitting room. It had been easy to sneak out as a teenager, something he'd taken full advantage of.

The smells coming from the kitchen were *wunderbaar*—meatloaf, if he wasn't mistaken. Every meal felt like a special occasion after eating prison food for so many years.

They settled around the table, prayed silently and then began passing dishes. He thought of Amos saying that a quiet night was rare at their home. All of the evenings at his parents' table had been quiet. They usually ate in silence.

When his *dat* had finished eating, he pushed away his plate and reached over to pat his *mamm*'s hand. "Excellent meal, Rachel."

"*Ya*. It's *gut* to cook for three again."

His *dat* nodded, then turned his attention to Noah. "How was your first day at the market?"

"*Gut*. Finished estimates for the bathroom and

canteen remodel. Apparently I'll meet my work crew tomorrow."

"Probably be *youngies*. Keeps our youth out of trouble if they can work and earn a little extra money." His *dat*'s gaze darted around the room, as if he'd stepped on a sensitive subject.

"I'm not sure a part-time job would have helped me, *Dat*. I had to learn things the hard way. No one's fault but my own."

His *mamm* fiddled with her napkin. "Will you tell them? Your workers?"

"*Nein*."

His *dat* met his gaze this time. "It's your decision, son. We would have supported you if you'd made a confession when you were baptized."

"I spoke with Ezekiel about that. In the end, we decided it wasn't necessary."

"Not necessary, but perhaps it's better to get in front of the gossip." Rachel Beiler was a strong and confident woman. She'd withstood all that Noah had put her through and never faltered. She'd faithfully made visits to Illinois once a year, even though it had meant only seeing him for twenty minutes at a time.

As far as Noah was concerned, she was the real deal.

They both were.

He hated that he'd caused them so much pain. Hated that he couldn't do a thing about it now, but he was certain that the best thing to do was move forward.

"Some people will talk," Noah agreed. "But they'll do that regardless of what I do or don't share."

"Okay." She stood, kissed his cheek, then began clearing the table.

Noah tried to help, but she shooed him out of the kitchen.

His *dat* sat on the couch, going over the *Budget* for the fourth or fifth time.

Noah stepped outside, walked to the barn, checked the horse and made sure everything was closed up tight. He didn't go back inside immediately, though. Instead, he sat on the old wooden bench outside the barn and studied his home.

How many times had he dreamed of being back?

Thoughts of this farm, his family and his hometown had been what had kept him going through those terrible years. Sometimes he looked back on the young man who had been caught up in drugs and dealing and it seemed like he was remembering a different person entirely.

He had been so young, so oblivious, so naïve.

He had thought he was invincible.

The counselors had been clear that their pasts would follow them wherever they went. It was something they couldn't outrun. It was something they needed to learn to carry, like a scar from a self-inflicted wound.

Noah wasn't embarrassed about his past.

But he fully realized that he'd caused enough emotional pain to the two people inside the house he was staring at. He would not be the cause of more. If that meant people wondered about him, let them wonder. In time, someone more interesting would come along and they'd forget about Noah Beiler and his missing ten years.

He thought of Sarah Yoder and didn't know if he should laugh or be irritated. She was certainly a curious one. She'd practically bit her tongue to keep from asking him even more direct questions. And when he'd said there was no use explaining what others couldn't understand, what was it she had said?

How do you know until you try?

Easy enough for her to say. She didn't have past secrets or sins to hide. She didn't need to protect her parents. Some days, Noah would like nothing better than to take an ad in the *Budget* and expose his entire past. That might make him feel better, but it would cause more pain and embarrassment for his *mamm* and *dat*.

Nope. He wouldn't be doing that.

He wouldn't be baring his heart to anyone.

Not even pretty Sarah Yoder.

Fortunately, he wouldn't be seeing her often because one thing he was sure about was that Sarah would not quickly let go of her questions. Another thing he was certain of was that Sarah would not be able to understand the mistakes he had made.

She'd always chosen correctly—stayed home, cared for her siblings, helped her father. She'd taken the straight and narrow path, and to Noah it seemed that she was so far down that path she wouldn't ever be able to understand the route he had chosen or how hard he was trying to right the things that he'd done wrong.

He would find a way to do that.

He'd find a way to do it alone, in his own time and without the counsel of friends who could betray him.

Chapter Three

Sarah woke early on Tuesday morning, put on one of her older dresses and a fresh *kapp*, then hurried into the kitchen to make breakfast. It didn't take long. Cooking for three was considerably easier than cooking for six had been. Plus her *dat* and Eunice were light eaters. Oatmeal with toast, a little fresh fruit and strong coffee seemed to make everyone happy.

It was while they were on the way to the market that her *dat* began to quiz her. "You're sure about this?"

"Yes."

"Because..."

"Does there have to be a because?"

Amos pulled on his beard, as if he were trying to hide his smile.

"It's not what you think, *Dat*."

"What do I think?"

"I suspect that you think...or at least hope... that I'm interested in Noah. In a romantic way."

"And you're not?"

"I am not."

"So why the sudden interest in working at the market?"

"As I explained on Sunday, there isn't much for me to do around the house anymore."

"So you're bored?"

That pricked a nerve. She could still hear Noah's voice saying *it could be they're bored with their own lives.*

"Let's say I find myself with extra time on my hands."

"Fair enough. I might have a more suitable spot for you than on Noah's demolition crew."

She waved that idea away. "Who knows? I might actually enjoy tearing something down."

"Yikes."

And then they were both laughing. It was a *gut* way to start the day. As they made their way to the market, as she looked at the passing farms—both Amish and *Englisch*—she accepted the fact that she probably was a little bored. Her family had needed her for so long, but did they need her now? She didn't think so.

She'd become rather obsolete at the ripe old age of thirty. It was a sobering thought—a frightening one if she were honest.

They walked from the parking area toward the main portion of the market. It was bustling with vendors and employees, even though it was still an hour before opening.

Sarah glanced at her father. "There is something I've been wondering about."

"I'd love to hear it."

"Why now? Why remodel during the busiest time of the year?"

"*Gut* question. Summer is easier than winter for construction crews."

"That's it?"

"People visiting see that we're upgrading the place, and that makes a *gut* impression."

"Why do I feel like there's something you're not sharing?"

Instead of answering, he kissed her on the cheek and hurried into the office. Sarah continued on to the canteen, waving at a few people that she knew, butterflies twirling in her stomach. How long had it been since she'd done something different? Something she knew nothing about?

Noah was seated at one of the large tables, and there were already three other people seated with him. When he looked up and saw Sarah, he did a double-take then smiled and widened his eyes in a comical way.

"What? I don't look like the construction type?"

He held up his hands in mock surrender. "I'm not going to argue with a volunteer."

"Volunteer?" An Amish teen at the table seemed to come awake. "I thought we were being paid for this."

"*Ya*, you are. It was just an expression."

Noah picked up his pen, dropped it, then nearly knocked over his coffee. He clearly seemed rattled by her presence. Sarah wondered why that would be. She hoped he didn't think that her *dat* had sent her to keep an eye on him. She'd have to clear that up as soon as they had a private moment.

His other three workers all looked to be under eighteen. Fortunately for her, at least one of the group was female. She was relieved to not be the only woman on the crew.

Noah checked his watch, then nodded in approval. "You're all here on time. That's *gut*. I'm looking forward to working with each of you." His eyes darted to Sarah and then away again.

He cleared his throat. "Perhaps we should begin by introducing ourselves."

"Okay. I'm Andrew… Andrew Gingerich. I'm seventeen and Amish." This earned him a laugh since it was quite obvious he was Amish. He was wearing suspenders and had his hair cut straight and short. "I worked here last summer cleaning out auction stalls. This sounded better than that, so…"

As his words trailed away, he jabbed the *Englisch* boy in the side with his elbow.

"Right. I'm Stanley Cook. I'm not Amish." Again, more laughter. "I earned all my credits in high school during the last semester, so I'm kind of at loose ends right now."

Andrew tossed his friend a knowing smile.

"Meaning his parents want him to go to college, but he isn't so keen on it."

Andrew raised his hand and Stanley slapped his palm.

"We're neighbors and best friends," Stanley explained. "So, yeah. He's right."

The group fell silent, and Noah nodded to the other female at the table.

"I'm Deborah Lapp, also Amish." She tugged on her *kapp* string as if to prove the fact. "I've tried a few different jobs. None seemed right."

She shrugged and turned to Sarah.

"Oh. I'm Sarah Yoder. My *dat* owns the place, but that's not why I'm here. Noah was describing his project, and it sounded like fun. I've always wanted to try my hand at tearing stuff up."

Which again earned a laugh. It seemed to Sarah like they were a good crew and that they would all get along.

"Let's all keep an eye on her when she has a hammer in her hand." Noah grinned broadly. "I'm Noah Beiler. Amos hired me on a temporary basis to remodel parts of the market. Our first two jobs are this canteen and the visitor bathrooms." He told them what he planned to do, how long he thought it would take and how they'd begin.

Sarah found herself getting caught up in his vision.

This could actually be fun.

This could be exactly what she needed.

"We'll start today in the men's bathroom. Gideon has already posted signs saying that it's closed for renovation and directing guests to the other facilities here on the property."

"I saw a row of porta-pottys as I walked in," Andrew said.

"*Ya*. Amos provided those as well. Today we'll begin by taking out fixtures, mirrors…really anything attached to the walls. The tiles are going to be replaced so we'll need to remove those as well. Hopefully by Thursday, or Friday at the latest, we can begin painting."

He handed out assignments, then told the group to meet him at the jobsite in fifteen minutes.

The other three workers yawned and shuffled off to get coffee and a sweet roll from the canteen.

"Not hungry?"

Sarah jumped at the sound of Noah's voice so close. "I already ate at home."

"Same." He nodded toward the two young men and young woman at the canteen counter. "Those three look barely awake."

"Young enough to have a lot of energy, though. I think you have a *gut* work crew."

"Why are you here, Sarah?" His voice was suddenly serious.

Well, well, well. So Noah Beiler didn't like being the one who didn't have answers.

"Maybe I was looking for a summer job, and your work crew just happened to be available."

"Is that the truth?"

"I only said maybe…"

"You're evading the question, Sarah."

"Hmm. Who else standing in this canteen does that?" She smiled at him sweetly. If he wanted to make an issue out of her working for him, she didn't mind. It wasn't as if he could fire her since her *dat* owned the place.

"It's going to get messy."

"I'm fine with messy."

"Might get your hands calloused."

"You're worried about my hands?"

"I'm sure there are other things you'd rather be doing."

"Actually, there aren't."

When he sighed heavily, she added, "Your project did sound like fun. I was being honest when I shared why I'm here. And I'll be a *gut* worker, Noah. You don't have to worry about that."

"Oh, I'm sure you will be."

"What's the problem then?"

"No problem. Just surprised, is all." He turned and strode out of the canteen.

Sarah stood there watching him. She wasn't aware that young Deborah Lapp had rejoined her until the girl spoke. "How come I've never met him before?"

"He's been away."

"Where?"

Sarah shrugged and changed the subject. "Are you looking forward to demolishing a bathroom?"

"Definitely. Anything would be better than working at the cheese shop. I put on at least fifteen pounds since the new year. I was hoping this job would help me slim down."

"You're beautiful as you are, Deborah. And I'm thinking that you and I are going to have a *gut* time popping off tiles and knocking down walls."

"We get to knock down a wall?" This from Andrew Gingerich, who had walked up with Stanley Cook. It was plain that they were the best of friends, which was one of the things that Sarah loved about Shipshewana.

What a merry little crew they made.

And if things worked out just right, somewhere between demolition and reconstruction, she would learn a few things about Noah Beiler. One thing she knew for certain was that he wasn't going to get rid of her as easily as he hoped. And why would he want to? She was a *gut* worker.

He'd probably rather do the entire job alone.

But that wasn't going to happen.

They were a crew, a group, sort of like a small community. And whether Noah wanted to or not, Sarah suspected that over the next few weeks they would get to know one another very well.

Tuesday, Wednesday and Thursday were *gut* days at work. They made excellent progress on the bathroom remodel. Noah's crew worked well together—serious when they needed to be, quick to do what he asked, and they seemed to enjoy one another's company.

Yes, the first week was going better than he could have hoped. Noah's muscles ached, but in a good way. He was pleasantly exhausted, lying in his bed in his parents' house, with a full stomach after a homemade dinner.

Outside the open window he could hear a slight breeze rustle the leaves of the trees, the call of night birds, even the clip-clop of horse hooves on the road. Must be a *youngie* headed home after a date. Who else would be out this late?

He flopped over onto his left side. The old mattress felt like the height of luxury after so many years of sleeping on a thin pad in his prison cell.

How many times had he longed for fresh air and the sounds of country life to lull him to sleep?

He rolled onto his back and stared at the ceiling.

Noah had spent many nights bargaining with God, making promises if only He would allow him to return home, give him one more chance, let him begin again.

And God had been faithful.

So why wasn't he happy?

Why was he wide awake after a hard day's work?

He sat up, scrubbed his hands across his face

and pulled on his pants and a T-shirt. He'd learned long ago that *trying harder* did not result in sleep. The prison he'd been assigned to had followed a strict lights-out policy. If you couldn't sleep, your choices were sitting in the dark or lying in the dark. He'd spent many dark hours doing sit-ups and push-ups on the floor of his cell, hoping it would use up some of the restless energy coursing through his body.

Now his body was exhausted, but his mind wouldn't stop turning over the events of the week. He padded into the kitchen, poured himself a glass of milk and fetched two of the oatmeal raisin cookies his *mamm* had baked that day, then took them out to the front porch.

The counselors at the prison had been quite good.

They'd worked at length with the inmates about to be paroled. Cautioned them against unreasonable expectations. Warned them that 77 percent of released prisoners were re-arrested within five years. Reminded them that recently released prisoners had a significantly higher mortality rate than the general population.

Noah was determined to not be one of those statistics.

He had no desire to use drugs, sell drugs, or be in the vicinity of anyone who did either of those things.

But the expectation thing…he thought he might

be rubbing up against that. His heart seemed to have been expecting something that hadn't yet occurred. As he settled into the rocking chair on the front porch, he munched on a cookie and tried to figure out what exactly was bothering him. He honestly couldn't think of a thing. His parents were supportive. Home was a welcoming and tranquil place. He had a good job, and a good work crew.

Work crew.

Sarah Yoder.

He was unaware he'd groaned until his *mamm* walked out onto the porch.

"Are the cookies that bad?"

"The cookies are *wunderbaar*."

She patted him on the shoulder, then hesitated near the rocking chair next to his. "Mind if I join you?"

"Of course not."

She didn't question why he was there. Didn't push or pry.

"Thought you'd be sound asleep what with all the washing, cooking and housecleaning you do around this place."

"Sleep can be an elusive thing, especially when you're a woman my age."

He thought he could hear the smile behind those words. His parents were aging gracefully, and he was grateful for that. They didn't complain about their aches or reminisce about the good ol' days.

They didn't dwell on what might have been.

As if she could read his thoughts, his *mamm* said, "All we ever wanted was you home. I have that now, and I'm content. But some nights...well, some nights my mind hasn't quite caught up with what my heart is telling it."

"I'm sorry, *Mamm*. Sorry for all I put you through. Sorry for causing you so much heart-ache."

"Oh, Noah." She reached over and patted his hand. "You can stop apologizing. What's done is done."

"It was difficult though—on you and *Dat*."

"Sure and certain it was, as it must have been on you. This family has been through a storm, but we're still standing."

"I suppose."

"Ours was a unique kind of heartache, at least for an Amish family. Not to say others haven't been incarcerated, but your situation was more severe than most."

"The judge was determined to make an example of me."

"And if your situation warned others off the same path, then there is some value in that. Not that it offsets the years we lost."

"Right."

They continued sitting in silence. Noah became

aware of the stars, the sliver of moon, the sound of the rocker creaking softly against the wooden floor of the porch.

Her voice was soft when she finally asked, "Want to talk about it?"

"About what?"

"Whatever's keeping you awake."

"Maybe my mind hasn't caught up with what my heart is telling it."

"Maybe so."

But Noah realized that he'd spent too many years keeping things to himself, too many years allowing his worries and fears, hopes and dreams to rattle around in his own brain. He was grateful for his parents and that he could speak openly to them.

"I have everything I wanted, everything I dreamed of when I was in prison—a home, the love of my family, a good community and now an excellent job. So why do I still feel restless?"

"Are you afraid you might lose it all?"

"*Nein.* I truly believe I will never step outside the law again."

"Is the job that Amos gave you to your liking?"

"Actually, it is." He laughed, thinking of his work crew, thinking of Sarah Yoder with drywall dust spotting her *kapp* and dirt smudged on her nose. "I have a *gut* work crew. Three youngies and Sarah Yoder."

"Sarah? She's a bit old for a work crew."

"My thinking, exactly."

His *mamm* was silent for a moment before offering, "They're a *gut* family, the Yoders. It's easy to forget the difficulties Amos endured."

"His *fraa* dying?"

"Yes, that was part of it. But also raising five girls on his own. It couldn't have been easy. I suspect, as the oldest of the children, that Sarah took on the role of mothering the younger girls."

"I guess."

"With Becca, Bethany and Ada married, she might be feeling put out to pasture."

"I don't follow."

"In our culture, a woman's value is closely tied to her family—raising children, being a helpmate to her husband, caring for a home."

"Not every woman follows that pattern. Becca still volunteers for MDS. Ada works at the SPCA."

"Amos's girls are very independent, it's true. Sarah's your age, right?"

"*Ya*. Nearly thirty-one."

"But the only one left at home, the only sibling for her to care for is Eunice."

"And Amos."

"Right. For most Amish women, as the youngest is leaving, the oldest is having *bopplin*. Sarah's hardly old enough to be a *grossmammi*."

"She's not too old to marry."

"True, but her options would be few in that area as well. Most of our men marry young. As for the widowers, perhaps she's had enough of raising children that aren't hers."

Noah almost laughed out loud at the thought of Sarah feeling like a *grossmammi*. She was so young, so full of energy. Her whole life was in front of her.

As was his.

"I hadn't thought of it that way," he admitted. "She's a *gut* addition to my work crew, even if she is older. Perhaps she simply wanted off the farm for the summer."

He didn't add that she was oddly curious about his past. He supposed most people were, and Sarah was simply honest enough to be open about it.

"Think I'll try to get some sleep." His *mamm* stood, kissed his cheek, then said, "Give yourself time to adjust, son. Give your mind time to catch up with your heart."

He stayed on the porch another half hour, studying the night sky, thinking of all he had to be grateful for and wondering what he was going to do about Sarah Yoder.

Chapter Four

By Friday, Sarah was sore in places she hadn't realized she could be sore.

"It's not as if you just sat around the house before," Eunice said. "You've always been a hard worker."

"Yes, but you use different muscles to remodel a bathroom."

"Are you enjoying it?"

"Strangely, I am."

Eunice grinned. "You sound surprised."

"To be honest, the work wasn't the reason I asked to be assigned to Noah's crew."

Eunice smiled broadly.

"*Nein.* Don't even go there. There's nothing romantic about popping up tiles or pulling out toilets. I didn't even know a toilet could be pulled out, but apparently the ones in the bathrooms we're remodeling had been there since the opening of the market."

"New toilets are better?"

"More water efficient."

"If you didn't join because you long to learn to remodel, why did you?"

Sarah hadn't admitted this to anyone. She knew she could trust Eunice. So, why did it feel so hard to confess her true motivation?

Eunice mimed buttoning her lips closed, then waited.

"Right. So it is because of Noah, but not for the reasons you think. He's so closed up. So mysterious. And it's only causing people to gossip more about his past."

"When did you start paying attention to people gossiping?"

"I don't. I mean, I don't believe a word they say, but I hate to hear them do it."

"But you did hear someone?"

"Ya."

"When did this happen?"

"After church."

"Ah."

"And again at work. Not our crew. Our crew is incredibly loyal to Noah already. He surprises them with cold sodas and sausages on a stick. They'd pull out a hundred toilets for free food. Plus, he's just generally easy to work for. Not tense or bossy as some can be."

"So your work crew isn't gossiping, but some of our church members are?"

"Church members and a few of the vendors. I heard some people at the market talking about him. Then when I turned around to confront them, I couldn't figure out who had said what."

"Might be for the best."

"I guess."

Eunice had been sketching a new solar gizmo on a piece of paper. Now she pushed it away and gave Sarah her full attention. "You're saying you took the job because you don't want people—Amish or *Englisch*—to be gossiping about Noah."

"It bothered me, and I didn't know what to do about it. Somehow, in my mind, I thought I could get Noah to open up. Then maybe I could correct those busybodies who are spreading rumors." She realized now how silly it all sounded. "I guess I was hoping that I could crack his hard shell. That we'd become besties—"

"Besties?"

"I might have envisioned him spilling all of his secrets. Once they're out, people won't have anything to gossip about."

"Some people will always find things to gossip about."

"Right."

"Besties?"

Sarah laughed with Eunice. She might have been aiming a little high as far as her goals, especially for the first week of work. Who became besties in less than a week? What a ridiculous idea. She finished wiping down the kitchen, then hurried out to join her father when he pulled up to the porch in the buggy. The morning was cloudy and a light rain had begun to fall. She wondered what Noah would find for them to do in the rain. Could you paint when the humidity was 98 percent?

She needn't have worried.

They met in the canteen, as usual, and Noah explained that three of the crew would be painting molding that would later be fastened to the tops of the walls and around the mirrors. The walls were to be painted a very soft blue-gray, and the molding would be white. The person who wasn't needed to paint molding would ride with him to the hardware store in Goshen to pick out the new fixtures for the bathrooms.

"I wouldn't know a stylish fixture from an old-fashioned one," Andrew said.

"I'd rather be drug through a pasture by a runaway horse." Stanley shrugged when they all turned to stare at him. "What? I'm learning that I'm pretty *gut* with a paintbrush, but I hate shopping."

"Well, I like shopping," Deborah said. "But not at hardware stores."

Noah tried to hide his smile, but he wasn't entirely successful. Soon all five of them were laughing. Shaking his head in mock despair, he glanced at Sarah. "Looks like it's you and me."

"Looks like it is."

The Uber driver pulled up in a nice, roomy

SUV. Sarah and Noah sat in the back. She hadn't been alone with him that often—or really at all—and she felt suddenly awkward.

"I'm surprised you didn't simply order online."

"I thought about it, but decided some things you need to see in person."

"Like toilets?"

He nodded gravely. "Especially toilets."

Twenty-five minutes later, they pulled into the parking lot of a large hardware store.

"Wow."

"Yeah. Apparently if you're in the market for toilets, this is the place to shop."

They spent the next hour picking out sinks, mirrors, hand dryers, soap dispensers, toilet tissue holders, hooks for the backs of doors and of course—toilets. Noah paid the bill with the market's credit card, then arranged for the store to deliver all of the materials on Monday.

"I had no idea how much stuff goes into a bathroom."

"When you're updating a bathroom that was built fifty years ago, there's a lot to change."

"Did my *dat* realize the price tag for this remodel?"

"He did, and he's all in."

"All in, huh?" She bumped her shoulder against his. "You sound like an *Englischer.*"

"Let me shock you some more. I'm starving, and we still have forty minutes before our Uber is back." He pointed to an adjacent pizza shop. "Hungry?"

"Starved."

They decided to share a supreme pizza and each ordered a soda. By the time the pizza had come, most conversation topics had been exhausted.

Sarah closed her eyes and inhaled the *wunderbaar* aroma when the waitress set the hot, fragrant pizza in the middle of their table. She might have groaned when she took a bite of the cheesy, doughy bliss.

"I guess you didn't eat out much when you were taking care of things at the farm?"

"I'm still taking care of things at the farm, but you're correct. Eating out doesn't happen that often." Because she didn't want him questioning her reasons for working at the market—after all, *he* was her reason for working there—she turned the conversation's focus onto him.

"How do you like being back home?"

"It's *gut*. Everyone has been real welcoming."

"I'm sure your parents are thrilled to have you around."

"They are." Instead of looking offended or worried, a knowing glint sparked in his eyes. "How does your *dat* like having you at the market?"

"He loves it. Has anything changed since you've been gone? I mean, ten years is a long time."

"Not that I can tell. You know Shipshe, Sarah. The more it changes..."

Sarah smiled at his use of the town's nickname. You could move away from home for a long time, but you didn't forget the little things about it. "The more it stays the same. Say, have you thought of asking Claire King out? I heard that she broke up with her beau."

Noah choked on a sip of soda, sputtered a bit and finally said, "*Nein.* I haven't. Have you thought of asking Andrew Gingerich out?"

"Andrew?" She dropped her half-eaten piece of pizza on the plate. "He's quite young for my tastes."

"So, you do have a taste?"

"How did this become about me?"

"I thought we were having a friendly lunch conversation." He sat back and took another large bite of pizza, smiling at her as he chewed.

Sarah wasn't about to be intimidated. "I see what you're doing, and you're right—it's none of my business if you're dating again."

"Danki."

"Though, Claire is a very nice girl."

"I'm sure she is. Andrew seems like a nice young man."

"He's not even eighteen! I'm not a cradle robber, Noah."

"Hmm. Let me think. Who else is available and closer to your age?"

"Okay. I yield."

"Kind of uncomfortable, isn't it?"

"Having someone ask polite questions?"

"Having people poke around in your private life."

She couldn't meet his gaze at first, but finally she sighed and said, "I'm sorry. I really am. I just think if you'd grow some roots in Shipshe, then maybe you'd stay."

"Grow some roots? I was born and raised here. Not sure my roots can grow any deeper."

"I mean, meet a woman. Settle down."

"You think I need to meet a woman and marry or I might disappear again?"

"I suppose that thought had crossed my mind."

"I'm touched that you care."

"No, you're not. You're offended, and I already said I'm sorry."

"And yet, you persist." He leaned forward and lowered his voice as if sharing a secret. "Perhaps the issue here is that your *schweschdern* are growing up and moving away. Maybe you're looking for someone to mother, but I don't need mothering, Sarah. *Danki*, I have a mother. Plus, I'm a grown man. I'm doing just fine!"

Sarah choked back a reply, felt her face redden and refused to look at him. She deserved that. She knew she did, but it still hurt her feelings to hear someone say such things. As if she needed another person to mother. As if she wanted to mother him.

She'd somehow crossed wires with Noah Beiler, and she wasn't sure that there was a thing she could do about it now.

Noah realized he'd crossed a line when Sarah nodded once and became suddenly interested in her half-empty cup of soda. They finished the meal in silence, he left a tip on the table and they stood to go. The sun put in an appearance as they stepped out of the pizza place.

He tried to keep his mouth shut as they waited for their driver. He honestly did. But he wasn't successful.

"It's just that I think it's no one's business what I do with my personal life."

"You're completely right."

"My goal might be to turn into a crotchety, lonely old man."

"Everyone needs a goal."

"Or maybe I haven't met the right person yet."

That stopped her. She turned, hands on her hips, color high in her cheeks—more beautiful than he'd realized. "I. Get. It. Stay out of Noah's life. Done. You don't have to drive the point home any more than you already have."

Neither of them spoke on the way back to Shipshe. He tried to start a conversation twice—once about the beautiful weather, though it was still somewhat cloudy and wet. When she only looked at him as if he'd twisted his suspenders, he asked if she'd seen the vendor who was selling socks turned into puppets. Sarah simply shook her head and returned her gaze out the window.

She basically fled once they were dropped off at the main gate.

"Way to blow your first date, Romeo," Noah muttered to himself. Then he realized what he'd said and dropped onto one of the visitor benches. They had not been on a date. They'd been on a work errand. Did he want it to be a date? Was he interested in Sarah Yoder?

She was so opinionated.

So inquisitive.

But she was also a *gut* worker with a pleasant personality. Plus, she was beautiful. He'd known a lot of Amish girls—Amish and *Englisch*—in his life, but he'd never known one who had captured his attention like Sarah Yoder.

He took off his hat, squished it between his hands, then plopped it back on his head.

Couples walked past him, arm-in-arm, oblivious to his misery. His eyes caught on a family of three—mom and dad each holding a little girl's hand as she skipped between them.

Would that ever be him?

Would he ever be a husband or a dad?

For over eight years it had been an impossibility.

Was it impossible now?

But Sarah…

Sarah would not be interested in dating the likes of him. Hadn't she just tried to push him toward Claire King? Perhaps she fancied herself a matchmaker, but it was obvious she wasn't interested in him. And if she knew his past, that would be the end of any relationship. Not that she would be prejudiced against someone who had made mistakes in their past. He thought she was more compassionate than that.

It was more that she couldn't possibly understand what it felt like to make such huge, life-altering errors, to regret so deeply something that couldn't be changed, to know that it would follow you wherever you went.

Nein. Sarah was a *gut* worker, and perhaps one day she would be a *gut* friend. What she wouldn't be was a girlfriend or a *fraa*—not to him, anyway.

The sun dashed behind a cloud and a steady rain began to fall. As he stood and made his way back toward his crew's work area, the crowds began to thin. It was definitely too wet to begin painting the bathroom they were remodeling. Since there was nothing else for his crew to do that afternoon, he loaned them to the Barnyard Animals manager who had asked for extra help. As he watched Andrew, Stanley, Deborah and Sarah walk off under a cloud of bright umbrellas, he couldn't help wishing that he was going with them.

He missed being part of a group.

He couldn't remember the last time he'd experienced that kind of easy friendship.

Instead of running to catch up with them, he walked to the office and settled behind the small desk Amos had assigned him. Someone had pushed it into a cubbyhole in the main office—which was empty at the moment. He sat and began to plan out the canteen's remodel.

But as he drew and sketched and tallied figures, he kept thinking of Sarah and wondering what was going on with her. Perhaps it was time that he asked a few discreet questions about Sarah's past. Not that he would be prying, and he certainly wasn't interested in gossip. But if there was a way that he could help a member of his work crew, he would definitely want to do so.

He didn't have any personal interest in Sarah.

But as her boss, even her temporary boss, he wanted to help if he could.

It was what any good boss would do.

He wasn't motivated by romantic thoughts for Sarah. That would be foolish, absurd, laughable even. Sarah and the ex-con? He didn't think so. *Nein*. He was only interested in her as a friend and coworker.

Or so he told himself, as he tidied his desk then set off in search of Gideon Fisher. If anyone had answers, anyone other than Sarah or Amos, Gideon would. After all, he was assistant manager of the market, a deacon in their church, and Sarah's brother-in-law. Gideon might be the very person who would have answers.

Sarah was clearly curious about his past.

Maybe it was time to do some digging of his own.

Chapter Five

Sarah cleaned with energy and complete concentration all day Saturday. She scrubbed floors that weren't very dirty. Changed the sheets on all the beds. Washed five loads of laundry and pinned them to the line. Scoured the stove until it gleamed in the afternoon light spilling through the kitchen window. It was while she was soaping down the front porch that Becca caught up with her. Gideon had taken baby Mary to the market with him, which left Becca with a rare couple of hours to herself.

"I thought you might go with me to pick wildflowers." She stood on the bottom step, holding a wicker basket and smiling. "Why are you scrubbing the porch?"

"Because it needs it, I suppose." Sarah stopped and wiped the sweat from her forehead.

"Except it doesn't. Looks to me as if we could eat dinner on the floor." She smiled and held up the basket. "Come with me. You look like you could use a break."

Sarah waved toward the clothesline—sheets flapping in the mid-May sunshine. Dresses, pants, *kapps*. Aprons. Dish towels and sheets. She thought you could tell a lot about a family by what was on their clothesline. How had Noah's mother adjusted to having a son back home? More laundry, but less worry? How much had it hurt her while he was gone? Fewer pieces of laundry each week to remind her of the one person missing from her family of three.

"Are you listening?"

"Sorry. I..."

"You disappeared for a minute. Let's go walk."

Sarah didn't want to go walk. She wanted to keep scrubbing. But the porch was clean. The house was clean. The laundry was done, and suddenly she couldn't stand the thought of five more minutes in her home.

"Sure. *Ya*. Sounds *gut*."

They strolled toward the farthest field, which always seemed to have an abundant supply of wildflowers. Something inside her unknotted as she slowed to appreciate the yellows, pinks and blues. She felt the warmth of the sunshine on her face and the breeze across her brow, and the restless energy she'd battled all day slipped away.

"Sometimes I forget to notice what's right under my nose," she admitted.

Becca pulled a pair of scissors from her apron pocket, reached down and snipped a few stems.

"Here. Hold my basket while I snip. Wildflower picking is great for easing stress."

"I'm not stressed."

"You're something."

"What's that supposed to mean?"

"It means that I've lived with you—or within a few feet of you—for my entire life. I can tell when something is stressing you out. What gives?"

Sarah shrugged. "I don't know how to explain it really."

"Start at the beginning."

Sarah thought that she'd confess about butting into Noah's personal life, tell Becca about the gossiping that had pricked her soul. But to her own surprise, her thoughts and words took off in a completely different direction.

"What am I doing here, Becca? What am I doing with my life? Soon Eunice will be gone—"

"Where's Eunice going?"

"She'll marry as you all have married."

"Is she even dating?"

"*Nein*, but that's not my point."

"Putting the buggy in front of the horse, but go on."

"My point is that it's inevitable that she will court and marry. Eunice is beautiful, kind, smart."

"Intimidating too. Don't forget that. I love Eunice, and I appreciate her unique talents, but it will take a special man to even approach her for a date."

"The right man will see beyond her mechanical nature. In fact, the man she is meant to fall in love with will appreciate that about her. She'll marry. I'm sure of it."

"Okay, so Eunice marries. Why does that thought make you miserable?"

"Then it will be just *dat* and me here on the old homestead." The last two words came out filled with all of the heartache that Sarah tried so hard not to indulge. She blinked rapidly to keep the tears from falling. This was so ridiculous. What was she crying about? Why was she so emotional?

Becca studied her, head cocked, surrounded by a field of flowers on an impossibly beautiful summer day. Finally, she nodded and said, "Ah."

"Ah what?"

"Ah, I think I understand what's happening."

"You do? If you do, please share, because I have no idea why I feel this way, or what I'm supposed to do about it."

Instead of answering, Becca pulled her over to an old maple tree at the edge of the field. The maple was huge and broad and had been there for as long as Sarah could remember. They sat side by side, with their backs pressed against the tree trunk and looked out over the field of flowers.

Becca placed the basket half-filled with flowers to the side. "Do you remember how badly I wanted to go on my first MDS mission?"

"You always had a heart for helping others."

"Oh, I'm no saint. What I wanted was a way out. I wanted to live my life…apart from here. Apart from what I'd always known. That desire in me was so strong that it blocked out all others." She laughed softly. "I wasn't gone two weeks before I became homesick."

"Your first trip was much longer than that."

"It was. I would write letters to you all filled with nostalgic longing, then crumble the paper and toss it in the trash."

"We didn't know. Your letters were always filled with details of the work you were doing, of the people you were helping."

"Right. I wasn't ready to share my regrets at that point. Then I came home at Christmas and everything looked so wonderfully familiar and also so completely different."

"What had changed?"

"Nothing. Oh, it's true the Christmas Market was in its first full swing, but nothing had changed here. I changed. I was able to see my home through new eyes, because I had left. Because I had been away."

"Is that what's wrong with me? I need to leave?" The words filled Sarah with misery and a small measure of guilt.

"Nothing's wrong with you, sis. And you're not alone in this. Remember when Bethany suddenly wanted to work at the Market's RV park?"

"We couldn't imagine our quiet, introverted Bethany working with customers."

"And then Ada became an animal rights advocate."

"I thought we'd have to build another barn to house all of the orphaned animals she brought home."

Sarah realized it was easy for her to forget that her *schweschdern*—her married *schweschdern*—hadn't always lived a contented, happy life with the man of their dreams. Becca, Bethany and Ada had all struggled against their emotions. They'd all matured into the love they felt for the men they eventually married.

She wasn't even at that starting place yet.

She didn't have a man to grow into loving.

Noah?

Surely not. She barely knew the man.

Becca reached for one of the purple flowers and spun it between her fingers. "I think that maturing can mean questioning everything you've ever known, as well as wondering what your place is in this world. We've all gone through this thing you're struggling with. Why shouldn't you? And Eunice too? It's just that it happens at different times for each of us."

"I'm fairly sure I've missed my chance of breaking away from this place."

Becca reached for her hand, laced their fingers together and waited.

Sarah forced herself to voice the thing that circled in her mind so often. "The runaway bride has lost any opportunity to run away. How's that for irony?"

"Why do you think that you called off all three of your engagements?"

"Only two of those relationships were serious enough that the word 'engagement' was tossed around."

"You're avoiding the question."

"Oh, I don't know. I've asked myself a million times. The first time, with Adam, I simply wasn't ready. It seemed we'd only just found our feet after *Mamm*'s passing. Ada was only eleven."

"I was fifteen. I remember wondering if you had figured out you didn't love him. You never said why, only that marrying Adam wasn't the right thing for you and that you were happier with us."

"I couldn't leave you all, and Adam made it plain that he wanted to purchase a farm in Kentucky where his cousins lived. The thought of being so far away from you all and *Dat* was more than I could handle. Maybe I was just a coward."

"You're no coward. What about the second time?"

"My relationship with Joe was fast and furious. I broke up with him a mere six months after Adam. I guess he was my rebound romance. I didn't really love him, I was just afraid of never again having a beau."

"And Simon?"

"Simon was two years younger than I was. He was also immature. I thought he would grow up once we were a couple. Thought I could change him, which I had no business doing." She rested her head against the maple tree. It felt satisfyingly solid.

"And there's been no one since?" Becca's voice was soft, compassionate.

"Nein." Sarah again thought of Noah, then pushed the image of him away. She'd told him she wanted him to put down roots. She'd stepped into his personal business with all the confidence and attitude of a real busybody. How embarrassing.

"You're turning thirty-one soon."

"Yes. I appreciate you reminding me of that." But she laughed. It sounded so pathetic, so *Englisch*, to be having a midlife crisis. Was she having a midlife crisis? But midlife wasn't thirty-one anymore. It was more like forty-five or even older. And what did an Amish person do for a midlife crisis? Purchase a new buggy? Take off for a trip to the Bahamas?

She was being ridiculous.

"Do you want children of your own?"

And that question did what all the other questions couldn't—caused the tears she'd been holding back to stream down her face.

Becca pulled her into a hug. "Then that's what we'll pray for. That you will have a family of your own. You deserve that, Sarah. You will make a great *mamm* and a *wunderbaar fraa*."

"What if I'm already too old?"

"What if you're not?"

In the Amish tradition, the Shipshewana congregation only met for worship every other Sunday. As far as Noah was aware, all Amish communities operated this way. Church Sundays were for meeting together, hearing the Word preached, singing hymns and fellowshipping with one another. Off-Sundays were for home Bible study and then sharing lunch and fellowship with family or friends.

Noah would have preferred to go anywhere rather than the Yoders for Sunday luncheon. His own family was small—just his *mamm*, *dat* and himself. They didn't have any relatives in the area to visit with on off-Sundays. Instead, for each Sunday when there wasn't a service, they were invited to one of the nearby neighbors' homes.

This time it was to the Yoders.

Just his luck.

He knew that his *mamm* was looking forward to a day of visiting and rest, so after they'd had their morning devotional he went out to the barn and hitched their mare to the buggy.

The Yoder family was indeed growing. There

were the five daughters, three husbands and two babies. Plus Amos. Adding Noah's family to that mix made for a solid fourteen. Not too many, not too few. The problem was that he wasn't sure whether to avoid Sarah or go up to her and act as if he didn't know that she was the runaway bride.

How could people be so mean?

How could they call her that?

A woman had a right to change her mind, same as a man did.

She hadn't actually run away all three times, according to Gideon who had shared her history willingly. "She'll tell you herself," Gideon had said. "Just ask her."

But Noah had been too embarrassed to do that. Instead he'd said, "I'm just trying to figure out how to relate to her. You know. As boss and employee."

"Uh-huh. Keep telling yourself that, pal." Gideon had said that last bit good-naturedly, then gone into a long spiel about Sarah's past and how great the Yoder family was.

He ended with, "I'm not saying she's perfect. Try walking across her freshly mopped floor with dirty boots on. That woman has a temper that is rare but frightening."

"Why doesn't she date?"

"Date?"

"Go out with men. I realize you're married, Gideon, but surely you remember dating."

"Now that you mention it, I do seem to remember that." He'd laughed again. "As to why Sarah doesn't date, I don't know. Maybe no one's asked her."

They'd been interrupted then, and Gideon had to go address a delivery problem. So what kept looping around in Noah's mind was the last thing he said—*maybe no one's asked her.* He didn't want to ask Sarah Yoder out. He didn't want to date at all. It was hard enough coming back to town where everyone had questions about your past. He wanted to keep his head down and do his job.

And yet, late Sunday morning he found himself at the Yoder place, handing Sarah the container of pasta salad his *mamm* had made and telling her how nice she looked in her peach-colored dress.

When did he start noticing the color of dresses?

The meal was delicious. His parents were plainly enjoying themselves. Everyone laughed at the antics of Mary and Lydia, who were full of energy until they weren't. Somehow Noah had ended up with Lydia on his lap, sucking her thumb and nodding off.

"You look like a natural *dat*," Ada said, plopping down beside him and adjusting Mary on her own lap. "Nice of you to give Bethany and Aaron a break."

"It's nothing that grand. I think this little one just happened to run out of steam when she was standing next to me, then she leaned against my legs and well… I couldn't have her falling asleep on the ground."

"These two girls are like two peanuts in a dish."

"Peas in a pod?"

"They do everything together. Even nap." Ada looked down at her niece and ran a finger along the little girl's cheek. "I hope to have one of these of my own one day."

"Do you now?"

"We're working on it." She laughed, then turned somber. "Say, Noah. Would you do me a favor?"

"Of course." He was learning why everyone spoiled Ada. She was simply too nice to say no to. She was also disarmingly honest. If Ada thought something, she spoke it. There were no hidden agendas with her. That was a pretty rare thing.

"Would you ask Sarah out on a date?"

His mouth dropped open, but no words came out.

"She's been looking a bit peaked. I think she needs to have some fun. You know. Something other than working at the market or cleaning here at home."

"Fun?"

"Recreation. Entertainment. Merriment. Wait, I've got it." Ada sat up straighter, nearly toppling Mary out of her lap. "Take her on the Barn Quilt Trail."

"What's a Barn Quilt Trail?"

"A trail of barn quilts, silly. I have one of the maps at my house. Someone left it on the SPCA table during my last shift. I'll send it to the market with Ethan tomorrow so you can have it."

"Yes, but—"

Ada waited, watching him, tapping her foot against the ground. Finally, she asked, "Does the parrot have your tongue, Noah? You look positively speechless."

"Huh." He was beginning to think that with Ada it might be best to simply nod.

"It's settled then. You'll ask Sarah for a drive and take her on the Barn Quilt Trail. I heard your crew has half a day off on Wednesday."

Finally a question he could answer. "*Ya*. The plumbers are coming to install the new bathroom fixtures."

"Perfect!" She reached over and squeezed his hand. "You're a lucky gerbil. Sarah's the best."

And then she was gone, and he was left holding a sleeping child wondering what he'd just agreed to do and how he could possibly back out of it now. To his dismay, he looked up and saw Ada standing next to Sarah, gesturing in his direction. Sarah looked his way and even from a distance he could see her questioning stance.

The runaway Amish bride.

Like him, she had a reputation of sorts. The mystery surrounding him was based on questions.

The mystery surrounding Sarah was based on her past decisions.

Decisions people wouldn't likely let her forget. Who would date her now? Who would be brave enough to move past the Amish grapevine?

He shrugged, offered her a thumbs-up and received a small wave in return. It would seem that he'd asked her on a date, and he hadn't needed to utter a single word.

On the way home, his *dat* said, "That Yoder family is a nice group to spend an afternoon with."

His *mamm* added, "Amos has had a busy life these last few years. Three girls married and two to go."

Noah cleared his throat. "I can see where you both are going with this, and you can stop."

"Didn't realize I was going anywhere but back to the farm." But his *dat* grinned at him broadly, and his *mamm* turned in the seat to study him.

"Have we told you how nice it is to have you home?"

"Almost every day."

"We're not trying to hurry you off."

"Hurry me off?"

"Take all the time you want."

"All the time for what?"

"You know." She waved at the world outside their buggy. "Everything. Life."

"Ah." He thought about dropping the subject

they weren't talking about, but decided that it was better to be direct. "I know what you're trying to do. I barely know Eunice, and Sarah would not be interested in someone like me."

"Someone like you?"

"An ex-con."

"That's an *Englisch* word. We have no word for that in Pennsylvania Dutch, and I'm glad we don't."

"If you say so."

"I do." Then she winked at him and turned back toward the front.

Knowing they'd hear about it through the grapevine eventually, he said, "I'm taking Sarah for a buggy ride on Wednesday, since we're off work."

His *dat* nodded as if he had suspected as much.

"That's nice, dear," his *mamm* said.

"It's not what you think."

"Okay."

"It's not a real date."

"Got it."

"Ada asked me to take her out for an afternoon, and I agreed."

"That Ada is a real hoot," his *dat* said.

"Sweet girl," his *mamm* added.

Noah wanted to drop his head into his hands. He wanted to insist that his parents listen to him. This was not a date! But he knew that the more he denied it, the more they would think it was the real deal. Best just to keep his mouth shut.

Why had he even told them?

He rested his head back against the seat and closed his eyes. Maybe he'd sleep, then wake and find this was all a nightmare. What would he talk to her about all afternoon? Were they supposed to just drive around and look at barns? Should he offer to buy her lunch?

Ugh. It had been too long since he'd been on a date—over ten years to be exact.

He was pretty sure there was a lot that he had forgotten.

There was little doubt in his mind that he would make some ridiculous mistake, then Sarah wouldn't want to be his friend, let alone his girlfriend. He didn't want to lose her friendship. He didn't have very many friends. He didn't have any. Which wasn't anyone's fault. He'd been gone ten years. Everyone had moved on. It wasn't like he could show up at the rec center in downtown Shipshewana, play a few games of baseball and instantly become a part of a close-knit group of friends.

At least he didn't think it would work that way.

Wasn't he too old for that?

He had three days to figure out how to take a woman on a date down a Barn Quilt Trail. What was a Barn Quilt Trail anyway? He'd have to go through with it, but he was pretty sure that saying yes to Ada was going to be something he lived to regret.

Chapter Six

Sarah had thought that Monday might be awkward, given that Ada had apparently roped Noah into asking her to go on a drive. But if anything, Noah seemed amused by her youngest *schweschder* and the situation she'd put them in. "She's sending me a map, as if I need directions in my own hometown."

"So you're not angry?"

"Of course not."

"Because if you want to back out..."

"Are you kidding me? No telling what she'll come up with next. Best to give in now."

Which wasn't exactly what a beau would say, but Sarah didn't take his words personally. She had no doubt that Ada had meant well. Noah's attitude was the correct one—they'd simply make the best of an awkward situation.

The work crew spent most of Monday and Tuesday painting walls. Though the work area was a bit crowded with all five of them painting in the restroom area, it didn't bother Sarah.

In fact, it reminded her of when she was a young scholar and their group would sometimes all crowd within a circle of trees to tell stories. Instead of feeling uncomfortably crushed together, it had felt safe and good. That's how Monday and Tuesday had felt as they all caulked, taped, painted and put down new tile.

She thought the room was beginning to come together. It was amazing what fresh paint and new tile could do.

On Wednesday morning, they pulled off the painters' tape and made sure that the room was as clean as possible for the plumbers. The morning sped by. Everyone's mood was upbeat at the thought of having an afternoon off in the middle of the week.

Andrew and Stanley were going fishing.

"Say, Stanley. Explain to me again why you aren't in school?" Deborah rubbed at a spot of paint on his cheek, then stood back and smiled. "Better. Now what was all that about earning your credits early? I didn't realize that was even possible. Tell us the truth if you're actually skipping."

Stanley laughed. "Believe it or not, I did finish all of my coursework last semester. I'll graduate with the rest of my classmates in a few weeks, but I don't have any classes to attend."

"Which is a good thing, because we have fish to catch." Andrew raised his hand, which Stanley slapped.

"What are you doing this afternoon, Deborah?" Sarah was hoping that the young girl didn't feel left out. She needn't have worried.

"My *schweschder* is meeting me at JoJo's for lunch, then we're going to shop for fabric."

"New dresses?"

"One for each of us…two if we can find fabric we like on sale."

When the hands of the clock pointed straight up to noon, Stanley, Andrew and Deborah took off.

"You'd think they were happy to be out of here," Noah said.

"It is a beautiful, sunny May afternoon."

"That it is." He put his thumbs under his suspenders and worried them a bit.

She had the awful premonition that he was going to cancel after all.

"Say, I need to stay around until the plumbers get here. Might be another twenty minutes."

"No worries. I could grab us some lunch from the canteen."

"That would be awesome." He reached for his wallet, but she waved him away. "We'll settle up later. Anything particular you'd like?"

"I'm starved, so I could eat absolutely anything."

"Meet you in the parking area in a half hour then."

Thirty minutes later, she'd spread the sandwiches, sodas and chips out on a picnic table.

She sat there watching Noah walk toward her, and she wondered at the fact that this felt like a special day. After all, it wasn't a real date. Perhaps it was just that she was doing something different, something with a person her own age. It didn't have to mean anything other than that.

And then he was standing next to her, his gaze taking in the spread of food. He looked at her and smiling broadly. *"Danki,"* he said.

"*Gem Gschehne*."

"I could eat a moose." He sat down next to her.

"Sorry, all we have is pastrami or turkey. Take your pick."

Unlike during the ride to Goshen, Sarah felt much more comfortable today. Maybe because they were on familiar ground. Or maybe because she'd realized—after talking to Eunice and Becca—that she needed to lighten up a bit. That it was okay to be a little discontent, even when so much about her life was going well. It didn't make her ungrateful. It made her human.

They talked about the progress the crew was making. Spent several minutes discussing the auction of two camels that had taken place the week before. Shared stories about growing up in Shipshewana, how it had changed and the many ways it had stayed the same. It seemed that they would never run out of things to talk about. It all felt natural and relaxing and fun.

"Better get to this barn fabric trail." Noah

balled up his trash and stuck it in the sack the food had come in, then held it open for her sandwich wrapping.

She acted like she was holding a basketball, tossed it, made it and he proclaimed, "Three points! Nicely done."

As they walked toward his buggy, she said, "It's a Barn Quilt Trail."

"Isn't that what I called it?"

"Nope. You called it a barn fabric trail and to my knowledge there's no such thing."

"Ah."

"No one actually staples fabric to a barn wall."

"That would be odd." He held the buggy's door open for her, but she moved past him toward the mare.

"What's her name?"

"Beauty."

"She is that." The mare was chestnut colored with one white sock. She nodded gratefully when Sarah offered her a peppermint.

"Do you always carry those in your pockets?"

"Never hurts to spoil a horse."

"You won't get any argument from me or Beauty on that."

They climbed into the buggy and made their way out of the parking area, talking about the horses their families owned and just how spoiled most of them had become. She directed him to the first barn quilt on the map.

When they were across from it, he directed Beauty to the side of the road. "I have never seen this before."

"You've probably driven this road a hundred times."

"At least." He shook his head in disbelief. "Explain it to me."

"At its most basic, what you're looking at is the first in a series of blocks that are fastened to a series of barns making a type of trail."

"Who picks the design?"

"The owners. Sometimes it will hold a special meaning, a pattern that a family member loved to quilt. Other times, it's simply a color or pattern that has caught their fancy."

"And this block? What pattern is it?"

"This is called a Rising Sun. See how the triangles on the left make it look like a sun rising over the horizon?"

"Well, I do now that you've explained it."

They drove through the brilliant afternoon sunshine, pausing at barns boasting various quilts—first a Nine Patch, then a Grandmother's Cross and finally a Fruit Basket. An hour later they pulled in front of Sarah's favorite—a lavender, yellow and green square called Fox Paws.

"Mind if we get out?" she asked.

"Sounds *gut*. I could stand to stretch my legs."

They stood at the fence, looking across the small

yard area to the barn with the quilt square mounted on the side of the structure facing the road.

Sarah thought the entire scene would make a *wunderbaar* picture. The fence, the wildflowers, the sheep in the far corner of the field and in front of them the quilt square.

She folded her arms on the top rung of the fence and rested her chin on her arms. "I love this one."

"Wait. You've been here before?"

"Well, yeah."

"Have you been to all of them?"

Sarah started laughing and found she couldn't stop. It wasn't what Noah said so much as the expression on his face, as if he couldn't quite believe he'd been had.

"Yes, Noah. I've seen all of the barn quilts. I love them. Love the colors, the farms, the country roads."

"So, why would Ada—" He stopped, obviously at a loss for words.

"Ask you to take me on a drive? I believe my little *schweschder* roped you into a date. Let me guess. She told you that I'd been looking tired and needed a day away from work or the farm."

"Almost exactly what she said."

She studied him for a moment. "You're a *gut* guy. You know that, right?"

He blushed and stuck his hands in his pockets. "I don't know that I'd go so far as to claim that."

"You are."

"How do you know?"

"Because you're kind, and you don't mind giving up your free afternoon to please my little *schweschder*."

"She looked so concerned."

"*Ya*. Ada always feels things very deeply."

"It wasn't a wasted drive, though. I learned something."

"Indeed. You'll be ready to quilt before we've made it back to Shipshewana proper."

They drove another half hour then ended up at Howie's Ice Cream. Sarah ordered a chocolate vanilla swirl. Noah opted for a double scoop of mint chocolate chip. As they sat at a picnic table enjoying their treats, Sarah decided to take the plunge and voice what had been on her mind all day.

"I hope this wasn't a sympathy date."

"I have no idea what you're talking about."

"Seriously? Sarah Yoder, aka the Amish runaway bride, has no one to go out with so you take pity on her and—"

"That's rubbish." He said it so emphatically that she almost believed him. "You could date anyone you want, Sarah. All you'd have to do is smile at a guy, and they'd be queuing up to ask you out."

"Ha! As if there were that many available thirty-year-old Amish males."

"Wait. You're saying I'm a rare item?"

She focused on trying to stay ahead of her now

melting ice cream, licking the sweet treat before it could reach her fingers.

"We're in a similar situation, Sarah."

"We are?"

"Sure. Both of us are nearly thirty-one. We're entering a new decade. Neither of us are interested in dating younger people or widowed people."

"Fortunately, I can't think of a single widow or widower our age."

"And yet people expect us to be courting. At least that's the feeling I get."

"I don't know. I don't think anyone expects me to be in a relationship. I think I've become..."

"What?"

"Invisible. I've become invisible." She stuffed the remainder of the cone into her mouth then tried to smile at him. For some reason the admission didn't make her feel as bad as she thought it might. In fact, it felt rather good to put it out in the light of day. To laugh about it.

Noah was shaking his head. She suspected he was about to argue with her. She swallowed the last bite of cone, reached out and put a hand on his arm. "It's okay. It is what it is."

"What does that saying mean?" He took a big bite of his cone and waited.

"It means that some things just are what they are."

"You didn't explain it. You just changed *is* to *are*."

"True. Okay. It means that some things are no more or less than what they appear to be. Like this picnic table. We don't have to know the history of the table, understand the meaning of the table, analyze the construction of the table…"

"Looks like maple wood."

She pushed him and he pretended to fall over, then righted himself and grinned.

He tried to look serious. "You're saying this picnic table is nothing more than a picnic table."

"It is what it is."

"Okay. I get it. And you and I?"

"We are what we are." She couldn't help laughing as she said it because it did sound somewhat obvious and more than a little ridiculous. And then something occurred to her that she had never thought of before. How had she never thought of it until now? It was so simple. So obvious. So true.

"What? You just had a revelation. I can tell because you practically have rays of wisdom coming out of your eyes."

"Maybe our past doesn't matter."

Now it was Noah's turn to look stunned.

"You've been gone ten years. So what? I've been in three relationships and yes… I did run out on the planned wedding for one. But why should that matter? It doesn't define who we are. Not really. It's merely a part of our path."

"That's quite…um, generous."

"You think so?"

"I do."

She stood, walked to the trash can and tossed in her napkins. Then she used her bottle of water to wash the stickiness off her hands. By the time Noah joined her, she was feeling remarkably good about herself.

He stepped closer, close enough that she was tempted to take a step back. She didn't, though. She didn't really want to.

"You're saying we should live our lives as if no one is watching?"

"*Ya*. I mean, *Gotte* is always watching."

"But don't worry about the neighbors."

"Exactly."

Instead of answering, Noah did something that she hadn't even dared to dream of. He placed his fingertips gently under her chin, tilted her head up and there—in front of both *Gotte* and probably some neighbors—he kissed her.

Noah couldn't explain to himself why he had kissed Sarah. He was feeling bold. All afternoon, he'd been thinking about how pretty she looked and how kind she was. Then she'd started talking about their past, about the things that usually remained unsaid.

And didn't that take courage?

Noah thought it did.

He thought that she was courageous and beautiful and kind. And he wanted to know what it would feel like to kiss Sarah Yoder. It had been many years since he'd done something without thinking through the repercussions.

And he had not thought this situation through.

He simply acted on some deeply embedded instinct.

But when she stepped back and smiled at him, he knew it was the right thing to do.

She started to laugh, and then he couldn't help but join her, and though an older Amish couple threw them an exasperated look, it didn't bother him.

How could anything bother him?

He was on a date with a beautiful woman, and he was enjoying himself.

They climbed back into his buggy and had traveled half a mile past the market when he realized he hadn't asked her where she wanted to be dropped off.

"Home is fine."

If he'd thought things would be awkward between them after the kiss, he was mistaken. If anything, Sarah seemed more relaxed than he'd ever seen her.

He wasn't sure of the proper etiquette for saying goodbye after kissing a woman, but he needn't have worried. She jumped out of the buggy the second it had rolled to a stop.

"I had a great time, Noah."

"I did too."

Should he ask her out for Saturday? But she was already saying goodbye to Beauty, then hurrying up the steps and through the front door of the house. He sat there stunned for a moment. What had just happened?

He remained in a daze for much of the way home. He hadn't planned on dating a girl—a woman—so soon after returning home. But not everything went as planned. Perhaps this would be a *gut* thing. After all, a person needed to do more than work, go home, go to church, rinse and repeat. There was certainly more to life than that. Or at least, he'd spent a lot of time hoping there was while he was a guest of the Illinois State Prison system.

Maybe the gossip mill wasn't as active as he'd thought.

Maybe their neighbors would let them be, and they could discover how they truly felt about each other.

Maybe they'd be allowed to simply be two young people who had something in common.

He had unharnessed Beauty and was brushing her down when his *dat* walked out behind the barn, surprising him.

"How was work, son?"

"*Gut*. Actually, I only worked half a day."

His *dat* seemed to be waiting on something. When Noah had nothing else to say, he cleared his throat. "Heard you took Sarah Yoder out for the afternoon, which you'd told us about but then I suppose I'd forgotten."

At first, Noah thought he'd imagined what his *dat* said.

One look at his father's expression—half bemused, half curious—told him that he hadn't imagined it. That was when the anger and resentment hit him like a freight train barreling down the tracks.

Noah thought the top of his head was going to pop off.

He didn't know whether to hold on to the anger or to laugh.

Since getting angry rarely produced the result he hoped for, he put his hands on his hips, stared at the ground and finally worked up a chuckle. It was the best he could do. "The Amish grapevine is alive and well."

"It was nothing ill-intentioned, son."

"Oh, you think not?"

"One of your *mamm*'s friends passed you on the road. She was coming here to return a casserole dish to your *mamm*. She mentioned it to Rachel. Rachel mentioned it to me." He patted Noah on the shoulder, took the horse brush from his hand and resumed grooming Beauty.

Noah slouched onto the bench, grateful that they were having this conversation outside, that he could at least look across the fields green with recently planted crops.

"Prison was like that," he admitted. "You could have a word with someone during a meal, and it would beat you back to your bunk."

"I suspect those people didn't have your best interests at heart?"

"Mostly no. Though there were a few kind people even in prison. But here… Do you think the people gossiping about me and Sarah, that they really have our best interests at heart?"

"Didn't say anyone was gossiping. Just said someone noticed."

"Uh-huh."

"Your *mamm* and I, we like the Yoder family. Sarah's a fine young woman. Doesn't bother us a bit that you two went for a drive."

When Noah didn't answer, he added, "Plus, there's the fact that you're a grown man and don't need our approval. If you're happy, then we're happy."

And those words—that tender truth from his father that he had never once doubted—poked a hole in his anger. All of the fight went out of him faster than air out of a punctured balloon.

"We had a *gut* time," he admitted, joining his *dat* beside the mare, taking the brush from his hand, motioning toward the house. "I'll tell you both all about it at dinner."

"Ya?"

"Sure. You'll enjoy hearing how Ada tricked me into it."

"That Ada, she's a hoot."

"Indeed, she is."

"Guess I'll see you inside then."

"Sure thing, *Dat*."

As Noah released Beauty into the pasture and put away the grooming tools, he wondered at the fact that so many things stayed the same. The grooming brush was the same he'd used while growing up. The barn looked no different. The fields hadn't changed. Life here had remained the same. And one of the hallmarks of an Amish community was that they were a closely knit group.

He'd come to terms with being under a microscope while in prison. The guards needed to watch, for their own safety as well as the safety of those serving out their sentences at the facility.

His fellow inmates, well, mostly they seemed merely bored.

He supposed a small town as well as Amish communities were similar to a prison population in some ways. People could mean well and still be a bit bored. Anything new caught their attention. He and Sarah were a new item, a juicy piece of news. Didn't have to be ill-intentioned.

He could either respond to the gossip or ignore it.

Since he'd enjoyed himself so much, he was leaning toward ignoring it. Or perhaps…perhaps they could be more bold with their dating and that would put everyone's questions to rest. They'd turn their attention elsewhere.

He rather liked that idea.

Sarah was a *gut* person. She was fun to be around. She was fun to kiss. And what had she said?

Maybe our past doesn't matter.

That was an attitude worth exploring.

And just maybe, he was ready to explore it. Ready to step out of the shadow of his past. The Amish ex-con pursuing a relationship with the Amish runaway bride. It sounded like the plot for a romance book.

But it also sounded like something that might happen. They weren't marrying, only spending time together. If he had the courage to do so. If she didn't learn where he'd been for ten years. Because Sarah might say the past didn't matter, but people often said that until they learned the details.

His parents wouldn't share those details.

Bishop Ezekiel wouldn't tell.

The only other person who knew was Amos, and Noah had great respect for him. He wouldn't tell. He'd leave it to Noah to do so. But Noah certainly didn't plan to bare his soul to the woman. He was going to date her. Nothing serious. No disclaimer required.

He liked the sound of that.

A small part of him even believed it was possible.

Chapter Seven

When Sarah did something, she usually did it wholeheartedly.

She'd thrown caution to the wind in regard to Noah. She was "all in," as the *youngies* liked to say. When Noah asked her to lunch on Friday, she readily agreed. When he suggested they go to the river and kayak on Saturday, she cleared it with Eunice and her *dat* first. Neither needed her, so she said yes.

This week, their Sunday service was held at Benjamin Lapp's farm. She was aware of Noah sitting across the aisle and a few rows back, sitting with the other men. It seemed she could pick his voice out during the singing. She was hyper-aware of his presence, but in a good way. If she were honest with herself, she felt like a young schoolgirl again. It was invigorating.

During the meal, she cast a few glances toward Noah who was sitting with his parents. But she didn't have a chance to speak with him until lunch was finished. Noah walked over to where she was sitting with her *schweschdern* and their husbands and babies. Everyone waved hello. It was Ada who popped up and said, "Take my seat, Noah. I feel like I have tadpoles in my stomach, I have so much energy."

Ethan grinned, stood, and said, "Best take her for a walk before she finds trouble."

"Those two." Bethany rolled her eyes.

"Young love." Becca laughed and then they were all laughing as they watched Ada walk over to a swing hanging from the limbs of a white oak tree. She plopped down on it, then leaned back and smiled up at her husband. Ethan said something that made her laugh, and then he began to push the swing. Sarah thought it was a tableau of love, playing out right before their eyes.

Then she noticed that Noah hadn't taken Ada's seat.

Instead he looked at her and smiled. "Good day for a walk, *ya*?"

"You know, I think it is." She slipped her hand in his, ignored the teasing of her siblings and pretended not to notice the people turning their heads to watch them walk away.

"We are stirring up the Amish grapevine, Sarah."

"Stirring it up?"

"Like walking into a hive of bees. Just…pow. Walk right into it. Bees everywhere. Buzz, buzz, buzzing."

She thought of that, thought of what he was saying—what he really meant, and decided that it didn't bother her if the bees were buzzing. It didn't matter if people were talking. All that mattered was this moment and being with someone that she liked. "As long as they don't sting, I suppose I don't care."

"You're quite sure about that?"

"*Ya*. I've had enough encounters with bees to know that when they sting it hurts a lot."

"My *mamm* once tried putting honey on a bee sting. All it did was make me very sticky."

"I've tried toothpaste, baking soda, apple cider vinegar and aloe vera."

"And did any of those things work?"

"You'd have to ask the person who I put that stuff on. It wasn't all my own stings. I learned to watch where I was walking. But my *schweschdern*..."

"Let me guess. Ada was probably trying to talk to the bees."

"She did go through a period of thinking she could sing to them. Eunice manages to stumble on them the most often because she's the one working in the barn or around the water pumps."

"You have an interesting family."

"What about your family?" Sarah thought the question was harmless and discreet. Noah had not yet opened up about his missing ten years. She wasn't pushing him to reveal all. They'd only been going out for five days, but she was curious about his childhood.

"Since I was an only child..." He hesitated, as if he didn't know how to go on.

"Rare thing in an Amish community."

"Indeed. Since I was an only child, things were pretty quiet. I suppose I didn't get in as much trouble as say... Ada. Most days I was on my own."

"Surely you had neighbor friends."

"*Ya*. But they had large families so there was only so much time to play with me. I'm not saying I sat around and read books all summer—"

"Ouch."

"You're a reader?"

"I am, though raising my four *schweschdern* didn't leave a lot of time for such things. Lately though...lately I find myself reading quite a bit."

"Things are slowing down."

"Indeed they are. But we were talking about you. What did you do if you didn't sit around reading or find trouble with your neighbors?"

Noah nodded toward a path that meandered along the far west side of the Lapp farm. "Do we dare to head around the pond where the entire congregation can't see us?"

"We dare. Now back to your childhood..."

He was silent for a few moments as they walked along the path—the May day showing off all of its colors around them. Blue, lavender and yellow wildflowers to their left. Green crops in the fields. A robin's egg blue sky that sported a single white cloud.

It all made Sarah wish she could paint, or write well enough to describe what she was seeing on paper. She thought this was a near-perfect day. Something whispered it might be a day that she would remember when she was old and sitting in her rocker, reminiscing about all that had come before. This moment felt to her like a watershed moment.

Now was the before.

But before what?

Noah cleared his throat. "I had a dog once that I was pretty sure I could train well enough to put in the circus."

"You're kidding."

"I'm not. Libby was smart. She would walk on her back legs, turn in a circle, play dead, even roll over."

"And how did you teach Libby all those things?"

"I'd pretend to be a dog."

"You're making this up."

"I'm not." He laughed and tugged her toward a recently mown spot of grass on the south side of the pond. He dropped to the ground and patted the space beside him.

Sarah sat, her legs stretched out in front of her, her face turned up to the sun. Why hadn't she spent more days like this? Why had she felt that she didn't deserve to rest on a Sunday or take a leisurely walk or date a nice man?

She closed her eyes very aware of Noah sitting so close beside her. Aware of his breathing. Of his presence. "Tell me how you'd pretend to be a dog."

"I'd put a dog treat in my mouth, lie down with all four up in the air…"

She opened her eyes to see him doing an imitation that did remarkably look like a dog.

"And I'd, you know, roll over. Then I'd hold up the treat and tell Libby to roll over. She was a quick learner." His voice grew soft, his gaze lingered on something at the far side of the pond.

"What kind of dog was Libby?"

"Jack Russell terrier."

"Do you still have her?"

"*Nein.* She passed." His words were soft. An admission. A confession.

She felt a wave of sadness settling over him. Because of a dog? She didn't understand. Didn't know what to say. So, she opted for making him laugh. She told him about Ada becoming an animal rights activist, how much it had irked Ethan at first and how she had adopted more animals than anyone in the family knew what to do with.

"A blind donkey?"

"Yes. Her name is Matilda. They still have her."

Noah smiled, and she understood that whatever memory had been troubling him had passed. A group of *youngies* had made their way around to the opposite side of the pond. One of the boys had apparently found a grass snake and was pestering the girls with it. Their shrieks of laughter carried across the water.

She sat there next to Noah for another ten minutes. Not talking. Not hurrying. Just enjoying each other's company. Finally, with a sigh, Noah stood and pulled her to her feet.

As they walked back toward the gathering of adults, Sarah said, "This has been nice."

"This walk?"

"This week."

"I've enjoyed it too. Even if we did make the Amish grapevine top ten list."

"Does that bother you?"

"Not as much as I thought it would. Still, I suppose we shouldn't give the elders in our group a heart attack by walking up holding hands." He squeezed her hand, then released it.

"You could kiss me." She stopped suddenly. Her words literally stopped her in her tracks.

Had she really just said that?

But now, as Noah turned to face her, laughter was dancing in his eyes. "That sounded like a dare."

"I suppose it might have been."

"So if I don't kiss you, I'm a chicken."

"Your words."

"Wouldn't want to be called a chicken." Then

he stepped forward and kissed her—gently and oh-so-sweetly.

She hadn't realized she'd closed her eyes until he said, "Look. No one even noticed."

When she did open her eyes, she saw Noah was right. No one was paying them any attention at all. She smiled, then resumed her questioning as they made their way to the dessert table.

"Favorite dessert?"

"Anything chocolate."

"Favorite drink?"

"Coffee."

"Favorite—"

"My turn." He waved a piece of apple pie under her nose. "Can you resist that? Freshly baked pie?"

She snatched the plate from his hands. "Why would I want to?"

"Exactly. I believe there's ice cream at the end of the table."

They took their treats and their coffees to one of the empty tables. Sarah could just see Becca and Bethany sitting on a blanket, their babes asleep in the shade of a tall sycamore tree. Gideon and Aaron were standing near the pasture fence, laughing about something. Ada and Ethan had moved on from swinging and were now playing a game of checkers. Eunice was talking to one of her old schoolmates, probably about the solar pump she'd recently installed on one of their troughs.

And her *dat* sat with the older folks.

Sarah noticed that it seemed everyone else sat in pairs. Her *dat*, he sat alone. She'd never thought of him that way, as being alone. But he was. And if she were to leave him, what would he do?

Eunice wouldn't live at home forever.

One of the boys would eventually find enough courage to ask her out, or she'd ask them out. Sarah could practically see it all unfolding.

And her father would be left alone.

Could she do that to him?

"Serious thoughts churning over there."

"I suppose."

Noah offered her a bite of his brownie covered with ice cream. It was deliciously sweet. She closed her eyes and savored the combination of the two different flavors. Perhaps she should savor these weeks with Noah. She still knew very little about him. She was under no delusion that he was going to up and ask her to marry him after getting to know her better.

Nein. She thought that if Noah were interested in marriage, he already would be. After all, a man only had to ask. But a woman…well, a woman had to wait. Or so their culture dictated.

Sarah was pretty sure that she was tired of waiting.

It was time that she took charge of her life, chose a path and started down it.

It was time to be honest about what she wanted out of life.

And she was beginning to wonder if what she wanted might just be the man sitting beside her. The question was whether she had the courage to do anything about it.

Noah had the distinct feeling that he was walking into deep water, but he was powerless to stop himself. How long had it been since he'd allowed himself to envision a bright future? Even his return home had been tempered with the warnings of the prison counselors ringing in his ears.

But Sarah…

He hadn't expected Sarah.

He hadn't had time to envision all the ways it could go wrong.

If there was one dark cloud in the sky, it was Sarah's incessant questions. He knew what she was doing. He even knew why she was doing it. She was falling *in lieb*. At least he thought she was, and he thought he was as well.

She deserved to know his past.

But he couldn't bring himself to answer her questions. He couldn't tolerate having this rare thing—hope—crushed.

So, instead, he deflected.

On Monday they began working on the women's bathroom. Now that they'd completed the men's, and they knew how great a difference the remodel could make, everyone was energized to do the same again. To do an even better job. He really did have a fine work crew.

Each day at lunch, Andrew and Deborah and Stanley would take off to the vendor booths looking for some new food to try. Sarah and Noah would walk to the canteen or JoJo's Pretzels or the local sandwich shop. Shipshewana was showing off with all the dazzle that only the early days of summer could bring. Noah had forgotten so much—the baskets of flowers hanging outside shops, the curiosity of tourists, the knowing smiles of other Amish, the familiarity of being home.

Unfortunately, those lunches were also where Sarah continued to pursue her investigation of his past.

Sometimes she'd try to draw a casual parallel. "You should have been here when we first opened the Christmas Market. That was three years ago, I think. We had the most snow in a decade. Do you remember that? I guess Illinois had the same hard winter."

"I'm not really sure. Say, want a refill on your coffee?"

She'd smile and let the question slide.

But the next day, she would try again. "What was the Amish community in Illinois like?"

"You know Amish communities…pretty much the same from one place to another."

"The same?"

"Sure. *Kapps* for the girls. Suspenders for the guys. Buggies for everyone."

"Probably an oversimplification."

"Probably."

He continued to check in with his parole officer twice a month. Tanner Pike was a nice man who had been working with parolees for over twenty years. He did more than look at Noah's paycheck stubs to confirm he was working. He asked about his health, whether he was sleeping, what activities he participated in outside of work. And every time, he ended the session with, "What was the most difficult thing this week?"

Usually, Noah pulled an answer out of his hat.

Overhearing gossip about his missing years.

Learning not to overreact when a police officer passed by.

Dreaming he was still incarcerated.

But for some reason, when Tanner asked him that question this time, the truth popped out before he could quell it.

"Not telling my girlfriend about my past."

Tanner sat back, tapped the fingertips of both hands together, and studied him. Finally, he grinned. "You have a girlfriend?"

"I suppose. I mean, we've been out several times."

"Tell me about her. If you want, I mean…it's

not a requirement of your parole that you discuss your personal life with me."

"Not much to tell. I've known Sarah since we were in school. She's the same age that I am. She's smart. Funny. Beautiful."

"Amish?"

"Ya."

"And she hasn't married?"

"Nein."

"A bit unusual."

"Her *mamm* passed when she was young, and Sarah sort of fell into the role of mothering her siblings. I guess by the time they didn't need her anymore, there weren't many bachelors hanging around."

"And then you came home."

"Then I came home." Noah looked at the ceiling, the far wall, Tanner's framed diploma, the wedding ring on his left hand. "She brings my past up pretty often. Asking about my years in Illinois. What it was like. How I liked it."

"What do you tell her?"

"I don't. I basically avoid her questions."

"She has no idea that you were in prison?"

"Nope."

"Doesn't know about your drug addiction?"

"Nope."

Tanner had been leaning back in his chair, but now he sat up straight, causing the chair to squeak. "And you like this girl?"

"I do."

"When do you plan to tell her the truth?"

"I don't."

Tanner shook his head and waited for Noah to meet his gaze. "We've talked about this, Noah. Your past is yours. And you are not required to share the details of your incarceration with anyone other than your employer and the local police chief."

"Exactly." He felt the old resentment swelling.

Noah wasn't under the delusion that he didn't deserve the time he'd spent in prison. He'd used and sold drugs that had a high potential for abuse, what the arresting officer had called Schedule II drugs. He'd deserved every day he'd spent behind bars. But the details of his life were his, and he was determined not to let his past spoil his present—or his future.

"I'm not required to, and I don't plan to."

"So, you don't see this relationship going anywhere?"

"I don't know."

Tanner had never been one to mince words, and he didn't now. He leaned forward, and said, "You're lying to yourself, Noah."

"I don't know what you mean."

"Maybe you've convinced yourself that you're a new person—"

"I am."

"Okay. Maybe you are. I hope you are. But any woman who is willing to marry you—"

"Never said anything about marriage."

"Let's be clear. We both know that in your culture that's the only place this relationship can end up—marriage or over. Those are the two choices."

Noah didn't respond. He didn't have an answer for that.

It was as if Tanner had spoken aloud the thing that kept him tossing and turning every night.

"If it's just a matter of you and…" He looked down at the notes he'd been taking. "You and Sarah having a good time, a summertime fling, then fine. No harm, no foul."

"And if it's more?"

The question seemed to ask itself. Noah certainly had no intention of asking it. More? What did he mean by more? Was he in love with Sarah? Didn't something like love and commitment take months and years to develop?

"If what you're feeling is more than casual, then you need to tell her and trust that she will understand." When Noah didn't answer, Tanner added, "And you know what, Noah? If she doesn't understand, then she's not the woman for you."

Noah didn't remember what else Tanner said. He didn't remember walking out of the building and waiting in the rain for the Uber to pick him up. Didn't notice his hair and shirt and pants becoming drenched. He didn't even remember the drive back to Shipshe.

What he did remember was Tanner saying that he needed to tell Sarah the truth. That she would understand or she wasn't the woman for him. That in their culture there were only two paths for their relationship.

Of course, Tanner was right.

Which didn't make those facts any easier to accept.

Because Noah didn't think he could do it.

He couldn't lay out his mistakes and U-turns and consequences as if it were an old road map that he had followed. There was no way he could tell her the truth.

He couldn't risk seeing the disappointment in her eyes.

He didn't want to watch her walk away from this relationship, and he was fairly certain that was what would happen.

Chapter Eight

Sarah did not want a birthday party, but her family insisted. Of course, Amish birthday parties were by definition casual. They didn't rent bounce houses for the children or take a weekend trip to Vegas for adults. Sarah had heard of those things, but their way was simpler, plainer and definitely less expensive.

Still, she wasn't too keen on celebrating her thirty-first.

Thirty-one years old! How had that happened? She was in the adult phase of her life and had been for some time. She wasn't sure how she felt about it. She wasn't sure she wanted to celebrate.

At least the party was limited to family.

Sarah wasn't allowed to help with dinner preparations, and they ate early so they could all make a trip to Howie's. Dinner was fried chicken, coleslaw, baked beans and the requisite vegetable platter that she'd included with every meal since her *dat*'s heart troubles had begun a few years earlier.

Sarah made sure he went to his six-month appointments with his doctor, and she constantly fed him seasonal fruit and fresh vegetables. She rarely fried things anymore, but Becca reminded her this was a special day, so she didn't argue about the fried chicken.

Since she wasn't allowed to help with anything, she tried sitting in the rocker on the front porch, but that made her feel old. She tried walking around the farm, but it felt lonely. Finally, she settled for attempting to read a book on the old porch swing, but she kept staring off into the distance and losing her place in the story.

After the meal—which was delicious—they gathered in the living room where her three gifts were laid out on the coffee table. Her *schweschdern* gave her a new *kapp* and fabric for a new dress. "I'll even sew it for you," Bethany chimed in. Bethany was a whiz with a needle and thread. Her *dat* gave her a gift certificate to the local bookstore.

"Everything I wanted," she proclaimed. *"Danki."*

She noticed her *dat* and Ada talking, glancing her way, then smiling and dashing off in different directions. She couldn't imagine what that was about. She'd already had dinner and received her gifts. It took four buggies to fit everyone, and then they were off to Howie's.

When they pulled into the ice cream shop's parking area, she noticed there was a good-sized crowd. Well, it was a Saturday in May. *Englisch* and Amish alike were queued up at the window of the little ice cream hut.

"Hope we can find a table," she said.

Ada grinned broadly. "Oh, don't worry about that. We have it all taken care of."

Which was when she'd looked to the left of where they'd parked the buggy and saw the mare—a chestnut with one white sock. It was definitely Beauty.

Surely this was not a coincidence.

Which meant Ada or her *dat* had invited—

And then Noah's *mamm* stood and waved a hand. "Over here. We saved the largest table we could find."

Sarah wanted to melt into the ground.

She wanted to hide in the buggy.

Instead, she scanned the crowd for Noah, who was standing at an adjacent table with his *dat* and another Amish family. He saw her, said something to the people he'd been talking to and walked over to her.

"Happy birthday, Sarah."

"Danki." She tried to still the blush creeping up her neck, but she'd never been able to control that sort of thing. She was so rarely embarrassed that she hadn't thought it was a problem…until now. "I guess Ada put you up to this. I saw her talking with my *dat* earlier, and I was wondering what she'd done."

"Indeed, it was Ada's idea that we join you."

An uncertainty colored his face and halted his words. He finally managed, "I hope that's okay."

"Of course it is. I just meant...well, I hope you didn't feel like you had to come."

"And miss out on ice cream? I thought you knew me better than that."

It took a full thirty minutes to place their order. Her *dat* paid for everyone's treat, though Noah's *dat*, Gideon and Ethan each tried to press money into his hand. Sarah watched it all from the picnic table where she sat next to Noah's mom.

"Your nieces are beautiful, Sarah."

"*Danki*. Mary and Lydia are also a handful."

"Children are an inheritance of the Lord." Rachel smiled, but Sarah thought there was a bit of sadness in it. "One of my favorite Psalms."

"Mine too," Sarah admitted. "Did you come from a large family?"

"Eight siblings, but they all live in Ohio. We don't visit as often as I'd like. We do send circle letters. I love those."

It occurred to Sarah that she really didn't know Rachel Beiler very well. A voice in the back of her mind whispered, "She could be your mother-in-law someday," and she almost fell off the picnic bench.

"Is something wrong?"

"A mosquito bit my leg, I think. Anyway, you were saying..."

"I don't know what I was saying." Rachel

laughed, and Sarah realized she liked this woman. She was pleasant, she didn't take herself too seriously and she seemed able to enjoy life. "Oh, the *bopplin*. I was saying how sweet they are."

"I think my *dat* worried that he wouldn't have any grandbabies—five girls and no one was married. Then in the space of a few years, three of my *schweschdern* did marry. Becca and Bethany both had trouble with their pregnancies, but both babies were born healthy within a few hours of each other. I suspect, I hope, there will be many *bopplin* in our future."

"And what about you?" Rachel shook her head. "Oh, I'm sorry. That was presumptuous of me to ask."

"Not at all. I want children, but I don't know if they're in my future or not. After all, I am thirty-one now."

"I remember when thirty sounded old to me. Now it seems like that was just the beginning of everything. Funny how time can change your perspective."

Rachel looked up then, looked past Sarah and a smile bloomed on her face. It reached all the way to her eyes. Sarah turned to see Noah walking toward them, balancing two double-scoop ice cream cones and three ice cream cups. There was so much emotion—so much tenderness—in Rachel's smile that Sarah had to look away.

It was more than a mother seeing her grown son.

It was definitely more than the beauty of the summer day and the fun of a birthday celebration. That smile contained an entire world of hurt and worry and relief and love. Sarah had once heard that having a child was like having your heart walk around outside your body. That's what she saw on Rachel's face—the burdens and joy of having a child, all wrapped into one expression.

What had happened in the Beiler family?

Where had Noah been for ten years?

And when was he going to trust her enough to share those things with her? She'd picked up an old book at a garage sale the week before. Paging through it, she'd found a quote by Paul Tournier that seemed to jump off the page. "Nothing makes us so lonely as our secrets."

She thought that might be true, and if it was, why would Noah choose loneliness? Why would he insist on keeping his secrets? She couldn't imagine anything so bad that she would fear anyone finding it out. She didn't understand what he must be struggling with.

Did his parents know? They must.

Did their bishop? Probably.

So why wouldn't he share what was burdening him with her? Perhaps he didn't feel for her as deeply as she was beginning to feel for him. She didn't know. She certainly hadn't asked. One thing she did know was that she didn't think their relationship could withstand that sort of secret.

* * *

May melted into June, and June flew.

Noah's crew finished the second bathroom and began work on the canteen. He wasn't sure what Amos would have for them to do once they were done with that particular project, but it was a big one and would take them at least six weeks.

It was the last Tuesday in June when Amos asked him to lunch. By this point, he had a standing lunch date with Sarah. When he told her that he couldn't make it and why, she'd grinned broadly and said, "You're eating with the boss. Must mean he's either going to fire you or promote you." And then she'd nudged his shoulder and kissed him on the cheek.

Plainly, she thought it would be a promotion.

Noah wasn't sure how you could be promoted if you were the head of a seasonal construction crew, but he did feel that they'd done a good job. He told himself he wasn't worried and that perhaps Amos just wanted to catch up. That didn't seem likely since he'd just had dinner with them on Sunday, but what did he know?

Amos suggested they eat at the Blue Gate restaurant. "My treat. I heard they have *wunderbaar* Amish food." He laughed, then added, "Might as well walk. I plan to eat whatever I want—since Sarah won't be looking over my shoulder. Maybe walking will negate some of the calories."

Amos ordered the roasted smoked ham. Noah

finally settled on the two-piece chicken dinner. Both were served with mashed potatoes, gravy, corn and biscuits. Somehow they ate it all and still managed to save room for pie. They discussed the weather, the crops, the fact that Ada had learned she was expecting a *boppli*, and how the market had enjoyed the largest crowds on record.

"I've been thinking of expanding," Amos said.

"Expanding how? Where?"

"I'm not sure. There's an Outdoor Market Show in Grand Rapids this weekend. I'd like you and Sarah to go."

"You want us to go to Grand Rapids?"

"Take the bus up on Thursday night. Hire an Uber to get around while you're there. Attend Friday and Saturday. Come home Sunday." He sipped the last of his coffee. "Why are you looking at me as if I'm wearing my suspenders backwards?"

"I'm surprised is all. Why me?"

"Because you're a *gut* worker, Noah. I'd like to keep you on. I'd like to make you my property manager."

"Property manager?"

Amos tilted his head and waited.

"I'm speechless."

"Is that a yes?"

"Of course. Yes. *Danki*. I'm grateful, Amos. More than you can know."

"We're fortunate to have you working at the

market. As for the show in Grand Rapids, I've asked Miranda to reserve you and Sarah two rooms at the hotel adjacent to the convention."

"And you think that will be…proper? What I mean to say is, are you sure people won't talk?"

"You both are adults." He leaned forward and smiled. "And too old for chaperones."

"Yes. I agree."

"Of course, all expenses will be covered by the market. Think of it as a combination of vacation and business."

"Are you sure Sarah will want to go?"

Amos pulled several bills out of his wallet and set them on the table. "You might not understand the effect that you've had on Sarah, but those of us who know her best, we can see the difference. She's happier. She's younger, if that's possible, and I think it is. I'm sure she'll enjoy the trip."

"Okay. I accept then. *Danki*."

"Gem Gschehne."

They left the restaurant and were nearly back to the market when Amos said what must have been on his mind all along. "Sometimes when we're away from our normal routine, we can see things more clearly. We can make decisions that have been puzzling us at home."

Was Amos giving Noah his blessing?

Or was he simply saying get serious or move along?

Noah didn't have the courage to ask. He was

afraid of the answer. It was true that he and Sarah were now seriously dating. Still, it had been less than two months. Was he supposed to ask her to marry him? Was that what her *dat* expected?

He pushed those disturbing questions away.

The next two days were more busy than usual, and by Thursday afternoon he found himself standing next to Sarah at the bus stop.

"When was the last time you left Shipshe?" he asked.

Sarah shook her head and finally said, "Never."

"You're kidding."

"*Nein*. Unless you count the hospital in Goshen or the Essenhaus restaurant in Middlebury. That's as far away from home as I've been."

Her entire life had been lived here, taking care of her family. This would be her first trip away. Her first real break—ever. Instead of feeling weighed down by that, Noah made a silent vow to show her the best time possible.

It was only a two-hour bus ride, and Sarah stared out the window for the entire drive. She seemed delighted by the countryside, the *Englisch* cars, the names of towns they passed—Three Rivers, Kalamazoo, Plainwell. Her eyes widened when they reached Grand Rapids, which didn't look like such a big city to Noah but then he'd become accustomed to a large city during his time in Illinois. He'd been living on the street in Chicago when he'd first been arrested.

"It's so busy. I never imagined…"

"I wish we had time for you to see Lake Michigan."

"Well, it's just a lake."

"*Nein*. It isn't. Lake Michigan is the third largest of the great lakes. Its shores touch Indiana, Illinois, Michigan and Wisconsin."

"How do you know all of this?" She turned to study him, her gaze becoming suddenly softer, almost tender. "Oh, yes. You lived in Illinois. Did you live near the lake?"

"I didn't." He reached out, tucked a stray hair into her *kapp*, then kissed her. "Best get our things together. I think we're nearly at the bus station."

The station attendant called them an Uber. They were at the hotel in fifteen minutes. Her room was on the second floor, his on the third.

It was a week of firsts for Sarah.

First time to cross the Indiana border.

First time to stay at a hotel.

First time to be free of the responsibility of her family.

For Noah it was a week without the shadow of his past hanging over him. No one in Grand Rapids knew or cared that he was an ex-con.

He and Sarah ate breakfast, lunch and dinner together. They split up the conference sessions, then compared notes and shared what they'd learned. Thursday evening they spent sitting beside the hotel's swimming pool, sharing a pizza.

Friday after enjoying a Mexican dinner, they walked through the park adjacent to the hotel. And on Saturday, on their last night in Grand Rapids, they decided to take an Uber to the downtown outdoor market.

The trip was going better than he had imagined, and perhaps Amos was right. Because suddenly Noah knew that he couldn't envision a life without Sarah in it. He knew what he wanted, and he thought that she wanted the same. All he had to do was figure out how they could move forward.

He was struggling with this, with the *how* of things, when the matter was taken out of his hands. Noah and Sarah had been walking through the market for over an hour. After studying a sign listing restaurants, they headed toward a seafood place. As they rounded a corner of pop-up stores and vendor stalls, coffee shops and pubs, they nearly collided with two *Englisch* men. The two were rough-looking, had obviously been drinking, and seemed strangely out of place in the upscale dining and tourist environment.

Sarah was stepping around the pair in order to let them pass, when one of the men did a double-take. "Noah? Is that you? Noah Beiler, as I live and breathe. This was the mate I was telling you about, George."

George peered at him, tried to focus and said in an equally loud voice. "You mean the one you shared a—"

"Nice to meet you," Noah practically shouted. He moved between the duo and Sarah, hoping to keep her from hearing their words.

"Say, how've you been, buddy?" Stuart's words came out slurred. He'd plainly had too much to drink.

Or he was high.

And as usual, he was loud and oblivious. The six months Noah had shared a cell with him had been among his hardest in prison. It wasn't that Stuart was a bad guy. He was simply incapable of controlling what he said. In prison, that could be a very bad thing, a very dangerous thing, and Stuart had suffered beatings more than once. Apparently, he'd learned nothing.

"Whatcha doin' in this dump of a place? Bunch of wealthy, golden spoon, good-fer-nuthing—"

Noah stepped closer to Stuart and hissed, "Lower your voice and wait here."

He took a deep breath, plastered on a smile, then walked over to where Sarah was waiting. "The restaurant is just there." He pointed three doors down. "Would you mind getting us a table? I'll be along in just a minute."

"Of course." She looked worried, concerned even.

"I'll only be a minute," Noah reassured her. He waited until she had walked away before turning back to Stuart.

"Pretty girly girl," Stuart slurred.

"Too pretty for you, pal." George lifted a bottle in a paper bag to his lips and took a long pull.

Noah looked past them, confirmed that Sarah was out of earshot, then turned back to Stuart. "So, you're out."

"Two months after you, buddy."

"I'm glad to hear it." And he was. He didn't wish ill for Stuart. "Listen, I'm kind of busy, so I'm going to—"

"Has that one made an honest man of you? Or are you just out with her for—"

Noah nearly punched him then. He clenched his fist, pulled back his arm, and Stuart fell silent. They stood there, looking at each other and all the things Noah had been trying to forget came into sharp focus. The confined space. The terrible food. The need to be outside…to be anywhere but locked in a concrete building with a thousand other men.

He let his hand fall to his side. The last thing he needed was to get arrested, and people were starting to notice the little group. Or rather, they were noticing Stuart's drunken antics. He suspected security had already been called and would be there shortly.

"You need to go somewhere and sober up."

"He was always worried about me." Stuart slung an arm around Noah. The man looked dirty and his smell confirmed it.

George handed the bottle in the brown paper

bag to Stuart, who took a pull, sloshing some of it on himself and then on Noah as he pushed it into his hands. "Have some. It's good."

Noah held up his hands and took two steps away.

Perhaps some of Stuart's drunkenness had been for the benefit of George, because he looked at Noah and said in a nearly sober voice, "I see how it is. Too good for your old buddies."

"We were never buddies, Stuart. We were cellmates. And if you don't want to get sent back, if you have any sense at all, you'll—"

"Sober up. I heardja." He grinned and resumed his drunken style of speaking. "What's the point of being free, though, iffin you can't have a lil fun?"

Noah realized he was wasting his time, and Sarah would be waiting. "I have to go."

He turned and walked away.

Didn't look back even when Stuart hollered, "'Ats no way to treat a buddy."

He stopped outside the restaurant, tried to calm the rapid beating of his heart, and wiped his palms against his pants. There was nothing he could do about the smell of cheap wine or the stain on his shirt. He tried to emotionally brush off what had just happened and went in search of the woman he loved.

The hostess took him to a table on the far side of the room. Sarah was sitting there waiting, looking concerned and a bit lost. Looking beautiful and kind and familiar. Noah's heart lurched at the sight. He couldn't lose her. He couldn't go back to what he was without her.

"Sorry about that." He sat, picked up his glass of water and drank the entire thing.

"About what?"

"What?"

"What are you sorry about?"

"Oh. Stuart. He was obviously having a rough night."

"He looked drunk."

"Maybe. Probably."

"Who was that, Noah?"

"Just a..." He picked up the menu and tried to focus, but the words printed there made no sense. His brain was still back with Stuart. His brain was saying he should have punched him. He needed to give his adrenaline a moment to settle. He needed to calm down.

But Sarah was still waiting for an answer, so he said, "Just a guy."

She reached over and lowered his menu, waited until he met her gaze. "Who is Stuart? What did you two share?"

"I'm not sure what the other guy was talking about. George. Didn't Stuart call him George? Anyway, let's not let it ruin our night. What do you feel like eating?"

But Sarah wasn't looking at the menu. It was

pretty obvious that she was no longer interested in eating seafood in the outdoor market in Grand Rapids, Michigan. All of her attention was focused on him.

"You're really not going to tell me."

"Tell you what? There's nothing to tell."

"You're acting very strange."

"Am I? Probably just hungry. Lunch seems like hours ago."

He wasn't fooling her, though. When he dared to look at her again, her expression had turned to one of sadness, realization, loss.

No, no, no.

It couldn't happen like this. It couldn't end like this because of a stupid guy he'd tried to be kind to in prison. He'd worked so hard to leave all that behind. Up until twenty minutes ago, he was confident he had left it behind.

But he could hear, over the roar in his ears and the beating of his heart, Tanner's voice.

When do you plan to tell her the truth?

You're lying to yourself, Noah.

Marriage or over. Those are your two choices.

You need to tell her.

Trust that she will understand.

He set down the menu and steeled himself. He closed his eyes and tried to think of the best way to explain all of his mistakes to Sarah. He imagined himself admitting how much he'd missed home, how he had never allowed himself to dream he could find someone as beautiful and kind and smart as she was.

He opened his mouth.

But he couldn't do it. He could not risk losing her. This woman had never been out of Indiana. She had barely been off the farm. How was she supposed to understand what he'd been through? Prison life, jail cells, your entire future at the mercy of a judge. And before that—his descent into substance abuse. His time on the streets.

How was he supposed to tell Sarah all of those things?

How was he supposed to expect her to know everything about him and still care for him? It was unfair to ask such a thing of her. And he simply didn't have the courage to do so.

Chapter Nine

Sarah tried twice more to talk to Noah about the strange encounter at the outdoor market. Both times, he changed the subject. Both times, he refused to explain to her who those men were or how he knew them.

The ride home on the bus was miserable for them both.

Noah kept trying to bring up vague topics of conversation—how many leaf peepers would show up in the fall, what his next project would be at the market, even who was scheduled to play at the Blue Gate Theater.

She didn't care about how many people showed up for the fall colors.

She couldn't focus on the next project.

She'd never seen a show at the Blue Gate Theater.

Gideon met them at the bus station, helped load their bags and dropped Noah off at his house. It was while they were on the way home that Gideon asked Sarah what was wrong.

"Couldn't help noticing that you and Noah were awfully quiet."

"Ya."

"Want to talk about it?"

"I'm not sure how."

"Tell me what happened. Start there. If you want to."

So she did. Gideon had always been a *gut* listener. Maybe he could provide a man's perspective. Maybe he could point out something obvious that she hadn't been able to see.

But he didn't have an explanation for the strange encounter or Noah's reaction to it. "But I do believe he's a *gut* guy. We both know that. I'm sure there is a perfectly understandable explanation."

"*Ya*. I agree. That's not bothering me so much as the fact that he won't talk about it."

Gideon was quiet for a moment. The sound of Kit Kat's hooves against the pavement should have settled Sarah's nerves. It didn't. Instead, she felt herself slipping into a place of deep misery. The trip away had been so relaxing, so much fun. She'd felt free. She'd felt as if she did actually have a life of her own—a life that included a very special boyfriend.

"You know, Gideon, there are ten years of Noah's life that I know nothing about. He turned thirty-one last month, same as me. Ten years is a third of his life so far."

"Right. The time he was gone."

"The time he was gone. It isn't as if he went to live with family. At least I don't think that's it. He's never accounted for those years. Never offered a word of explanation. So when two drunken men show up calling him *mate* and *buddy*, I have to assume that he knows them pretty well. That possibly they have something to do with those missing years."

"Okay. Let's say they do."

Gideon was staring at the road, taking her situation seriously. He didn't laugh at her or tell her that she was being unreasonable. He seemed to understand her predicament, maybe as well or better than she did.

"Let's say he was gone for ten years, maybe involved in something that he's not proud of. He's probably afraid if he mentions it, if he explains, that you will end the relationship. It's plain he cares about you, Sarah."

"And I care about him."

"But…"

"But it's not much of a relationship if we can't trust each other."

Gideon didn't have an answer for that. They rode the rest of the way home in silence. Sarah tried to plaster on a smile for her family. She told them the conference was *wunderbaar*, Grand Rapids was a beautiful town, and she'd enjoyed nearly all of it. She admitted that there had been some trouble between her and Noah—a "misunderstanding" was how she'd phrased it, but she didn't go into details.

Soon a headache formed at the back of her neck, and she felt inexplicably weary. "Think I'll turn in early," she said.

She and her *dat* and Eunice had been sitting at the table, enjoying coffee and a box of cookies she'd brought back from Grand Rapids.

"Probably a *gut* idea. Get some rest and things will look better tomorrow." Her *dat* stood and kissed her on top of the head.

Tears sprang to her eyes, and she pushed herself to her feet, turned toward the sink, toward the dinner dishes that needed to be done.

"I'll take care of these," Eunice offered.

Sarah nodded once and fled.

She spent much of that night tossing and turning and finally writing in the journal that she only bothered to write in when she was feeling something extreme, something she couldn't quite handle otherwise.

The pages were filled with joyous moments—the births of Lydia and Mary, the marriages of her *schweschdern*, even the baptism of each of them. There were also pages filled with terribly sad moments—her failed relationships, her father's health concerns, the pregnancy troubles that both Becca and Bethany had faced.

There wasn't a single page that talked about

gardens or sunsets or pleasant dinners with her family. She supposed those everyday moments, the moments that made up the bulk of her life, were things that didn't need processing. But the celebrations as well as the heartbreaks had to be dealt with. She'd learned at a young age that in times of great distress or confusion, it helped her to write out what was bothering her.

The list she penned that night was a fairly short one.

I'm falling in love with Noah.
I think he loves me.
There's a part of his life that he refuses to share.
A huge block of time—missing.
I have to either accept that or end the relationship.

She knew, in her heart of hearts, that she couldn't accept such a thing. It wasn't the specifics of what he was hiding. She didn't care where he'd been or what he'd done. He was here now, and he was a *gut* person. How bad could it possibly have been?

But more importantly, mature love required trust.

She remembered how her *mamm* and *dat* had related to each other. Remembered hearing their voices long after she'd gone to bed—talking softly as they sat in the rockers on the porch or in front of a fire on the couch. She remembered her *dat* being upset about something at work and telling her *mamm* about it. She remembered her *mamm* crying when her parents had passed. Sarah had snuck down the hall that time, peered into the living room, seen her *dat* holding her *mamm* in his arms. She didn't know the details of those conversations, but she understood at a very young age that love meant sharing your most vulnerable moments with the person you loved.

Noah wasn't willing to do that.

It was quite obvious that Noah didn't trust her.

And love, without trust, wasn't a very solid foundation for a relationship.

Finally, she closed the journal and slept.

The next day they resumed work on the canteen area. They were popping tiles off the floor, readying the walls for a fresh coat of paint.

When Noah asked her what she'd like for lunch, she begged off. "I brought a sandwich actually. Think I'll pop over and see Bethany at the RV park." Then she'd hurried off before he had a chance to offer to go with her.

Bethany didn't work at the RV park every day, but she liked to come in on Mondays, which was the day that campers who were traveling to their next destination usually left. Bethany liked to be there to personally tell them goodbye and invite them back.

Sarah had no intention of sharing her own problems again. Gideon hadn't had any answers. She doubted that Bethany would. She wasn't even sure there was an answer to this situation.

But Bethany had gently encouraged her to talk about what was on her heart, and then her response surprised Sarah.

"I understand."

"You do?"

"*Ya*. Remember, Aaron didn't want to tell me about his fears or his past. He was afraid to talk about what it had been like growing up with a father who suffered from bipolar disorder. He'd certainly never expressed how he had to take on the role of an adult at a young age. And his biggest fear, the thing that held him back, was that he would have the same disease his father suffers from."

"I suppose I'd forgotten those things."

"It was a difficult time for us. Even after he'd finally shared his feelings with me, I think it still took a while for him to trust me, trust that it didn't matter, trust that I still loved him."

"But what if he'd refused to share those things with you?"

"Then I think our relationship would have been over."

"Right."

"I'm not saying your relationship with Noah is

over. Maybe it is. Maybe it isn't. But your feelings are valid, Sarah."

Instead of answering, Sarah allowed Bethany to pull her into a hug. It was odd, being the one to receive comfort from her little *schweschder*. She'd always been the oldest, the one to put a Band-Aid on a scrape or smooth over hurt feelings.

Later that afternoon, she went next door and talked to Becca who gave her the same advice. "You're not overreacting. And you're right to want what your heart wants. These feelings you're struggling with are difficult."

That evening at dinner, she shared with Eunice and her *dat* the details of what had happened that final evening in Grand Rapids.

"Sorry, sis. I had no idea."

"Not your fault."

Her *dat* had a more thoughtful look on his face, but when she asked him about it, when she asked him if there was some light he could shed on the situation, he'd shook his head. "I wish I could, but it's not my place."

So he knew?

Was her *dat* aware of details of Noah's history that she wasn't? Did he know about the missing years?

"I'll only say what you already know. That I love you, and I respect your decision."

It was Ada who offered the one piece of advice that she wanted to argue with. Ada had stopped by the market at lunch to drop off some jars of potpourri she'd made to one of the vendors. It turned out that Ada had a real knack for mixing unusual things together in a way that looked pleasing and fun. Pine cones with buttons and ribbon. Cinnamon sticks with dried orange peels and scraps of fabric. Her unique way of looking at things resulted in some very unusual and beautiful jars of potpourri. They sold like hotcakes.

"You need to tell him," Ada said.

"What do you mean?"

"I mean, you need to have the difficult conversation with Noah."

"But—"

"Noah could be in the same buggy."

"In the same boat?"

"We don't have many boats, but look. Maybe he wants to explain as much as you want to hear..."

"I don't think so. I asked several times—probably a dozen times."

Ada had stopped in the middle of the sidewalk as *Englisch* tourists stepped around them. She'd put her hands on Sarah's shoulders and scrunched up her face and said, "Ask again. Sometimes, the thirteenth time is the one that works. Tell him how you feel, why you feel that way and give him another chance."

"Give him an ultimatum."

"*Nein.* Explain that you need someone who isn't a closed oven."

"A closed book?"

"Yup. Exactly." Then she'd hooked her arm through Sarah's and walked her back toward the canteen. They'd spoken of Ada's pregnancy—no morning sickness. They'd laughed over Aaron's excitement—he was already working on a crib. Sarah was happy for her littlest *schweschder*, but she couldn't help wondering if she'd ever be the one planning for a family.

One thing was certain.

Ada was right.

It was time to have the difficult conversation.

Noah understood that Sarah was upset.

Running into someone like Stuart had been plain bad luck. He was hoping she'd forget the incident. So far, that hadn't happened. She'd spoken to him very little the previous day or that morning. Both days she'd had lunch with one of her *schweschdern*. The previous afternoon she'd left before he could offer her a ride home.

But when she returned from lunch with Ada on Tuesday, he noticed her watching him. When Deborah and Andrew and Stanley had left for the day, she hung back. His heart soared. She'd forgiven him. He could tell from the tender look on her face. She'd put Grand Rapids behind them.

"Want to go for an ice cream cone?" he asked.

"Nein."

"Pretzel?"

"I'm not hungry. I did hope we could talk for a minute."

"Sure." He waited, suddenly unsure now if this was a good or bad turn of events.

She walked over to their workbench. Picked up a paintbrush, then set it back down. Finally, she turned to look at him. "You know I care about you, right?"

"And I care about you." Why did those words hurt as they came out of his throat? Why was his stomach settling into an impossible heaviness, as if he'd swallowed a rock?

"I want to explain why I'm upset about what happened in Grand Rapids."

"Okay." He crossed his arms, the old feelings of resentment building in him. "But you know I wasn't the one drinking, right? That guy spilled his cheap wine all over me. That's why I smelled like a vineyard."

"It wasn't the wine. It wasn't even Stuart and George."

He winced at his former cellmate's name. So, she hadn't forgotten. Of course, she hadn't. That would have been too much to hope for. And she wasn't going to let it drop. She was going to beat it like an old, dusty rug.

"People are who they are, Noah. I don't know Stuart's story. I can't even imagine George's story. I don't know why they were drunk and wandering through the market. I don't want or need to know those things."

"Okay."

"They aren't my boyfriend. You are. Or you were."

He could literally feel the muscles in his face pulling his frown into a scowl. "Were? Are you breaking up with me?"

"Maybe."

"Maybe?" He fought to bring his voice down. "Because of a random encounter with two men in an open market in Grand Rapids?"

"Because you won't be honest about your past." She waited, expectantly. When he didn't respond to that, she shook her head and turned away from him.

He wondered if she was crying.

Well, he wasn't going to fall for the crying woman tactic. Sarah Yoder needed to grow up and realize that not everyone had the picture-perfect past like she did. Not everyone wanted or needed to talk it out. He could handle his own secrets, and he did not need to share them. Before he could put those thoughts into words, she turned back to him.

She wasn't crying.

She was very serious.

"If we are going to be in a relationship—what I thought was a serious relationship—then we have to be able to trust each other."

"You *can* trust me."

"We have to be able to talk about our past and our fears and our hopes and dreams. Or else what's the point?"

"Easy for you to say," he muttered.

"What's that supposed to mean?"

"Your past has been fairly perfect from where I'm standing."

"Perfect? You think having your *mamm* die when you're eleven is perfect? You think raising your four *schweschdern* is perfect?"

"That's not what I meant."

"Then what did you mean?"

The question sat between them, like a wall that was growing taller and longer. Like a wall that could keep them apart for the rest of time, and Noah had no idea how to scale it or knock it down. He needed to get control of this situation, but he didn't know what to do or say.

"What did you mean, Noah?"

"I was trying to point out that you have nothing in your life you're ashamed of."

"And neither should you. Noah, it's not like you killed anyone."

He literally jerked back. His voice, when he was finally able to speak, sounded nothing like himself. It sounded like some beaten and defeated animal. "How would you know, Sarah? How would you know what I have or haven't done?"

And then he turned and walked out of the canteen.

Outside, the day had turned stormy, gloomy, depressing.

He wasn't a bit surprised. The dark clouds matched his mood. How had he dared to think he could have a fresh start? People wouldn't allow that. Even the woman he loved wouldn't allow that. Fresh starts were a thing from fairy tales.

And his life, most certainly, was not that.

He drove home in a sullen mood. How often had he dreamed of guiding a horse down the streets of Shipshe? He'd thought of his hometown as an anchor, as a thing that would hold him steady against a buffeting world.

Now he saw that it was simply a small town.

Filled with small-minded people.

Refusing to change.

Refusing to offer mercy or grace.

Had he really dreamed it could be different? He pulled into his parents' farm and stopped in the lane that led to the small house. Other than the streets of Chicago and the inside of the Illinois State Prison, this was the only home he'd ever known. At a mere sixty-two acres, it wasn't a large farm. It was barely big enough to grow a sufficient amount of crops to sustain a small family.

It would never make his father rich.

It would never make his life easy. He could feel the smallness of it closing in on him.

The counselors in prison had insisted that he dig deep and find what had caused him to turn to drugs in the first place. He'd refused. He'd insisted he'd simply been a dumb kid who made dumb mistakes.

But maybe that wasn't true.

Maybe the expectations of his parents—no matter how well-meaning—had weighed on him. The path that he was supposed to follow had been obvious. Learn to work the land. Meet a woman. Marry. Have children. Teach them to work the land.

He'd felt that pressure coming from his parents, his teachers, even his church. He'd felt as if he'd had no other options, so he'd punched through the wall of his small town and embraced terrible choices.

A farm. A family. A simple life.

Noah didn't know if he wanted that future or not. He did know that he didn't want his past. No amount of pressure or limitations would push him back into the drug culture. He'd learned that lesson very well.

But was he willing to face this cookie-cutter future?

Was he willing to face a life on the farm?

"Walk on," he called to Beauty, and she took them to the barn where he unharnessed her, brushed her down, put oats in her bucket. He took his time doing those things, and when he was finished, when he'd closed the barn up for the night, he understood what he needed to do.

He might not be able to be honest with Sarah. He was convinced that she couldn't possibly understand.

But his parents knew his past, and now it was time they understood his doubts about his future.

Chapter Ten

The next two weeks were among the bleakest of Noah's life, and that was saying something. They were even worse than the months he'd been homeless. During those dark days, the drugs he abused helped him to ignore the truth about his situation. He and his fellow addicts considered themselves footloose and fancy-free.

Free of others' expectations.

Free of a nine-to-five job.

Free of friendships and family.

His years in prison had been a terrible time, but that despair had been tempered by the knowledge that he deserved the time he'd been sentenced to. Coming off the drugs, getting clean, eating three meals a day—it had all balanced the misery of his time in a cell.

That and the knowledge that he would one day be truly free.

He had been so determined to grasp that future.

So why did he now feel like a man serving a sentence?

His parents were of little help. They seemed to understand that he might not want to be a farmer.

"You don't have to decide now," his *mamm* had reminded him.

His *dat* had been more direct. "This farm, these fields, this life—it was all my choice. What I wanted. I never even considered being anything but what my father had been. When I was a young man, when I was your age, there weren't as many opportunities. I've been happy here, and yes—there was a time when I dreamed of you following in my footsteps."

Noah had sank lower in his chair.

"Now my wish for you is that you find the thing that brings satisfaction at the end of the day. The thing that you look forward to doing each morning. Do you enjoy your work at the market?"

"*Ya*, I do. Renovating things feels natural to me, or maybe it's that I can relate so well to what I'm doing. I like seeing something old and turning it into something new. And I'm *gut* at it. At least I think I am."

"Then follow that dream, son. See if you can turn it from a job into a vocation. Your *mamm* and I will support you in whatever choice you make."

It was a relief to hear those words—a relief to have the difficult conversation he'd been dreading. His parents were very understanding about what work he would do. But in regard to his personal relationships, they seemed puzzled. If anything, that made him feel worse. They asked him what had happened between him and Sarah.

He'd responded simply, "Didn't work out," and he left to muck out the horse stalls.

The sadness and disappointment that emanated from them was almost more than he could bear. He'd let them down—again. They'd probably been planning the wedding and dreaming of grandchildren. Sketching out an addition to the small house.

It wasn't going to happen. Not with Sarah. Probably not with anyone. He didn't see how to climb over the hurdle of his past. He didn't think it would be fair to ask her to embrace his baggage.

Amos tried to broach the subject once, but Noah had stopped him as soon as he realized the conversation was about Sarah. "I'm sorry, Amos. I don't want to talk about this, but I will say that she's better off without me."

"I don't believe that's true."

Noah didn't have an answer to that. Amos might know his history, undoubtedly understood how much time he'd spent in prison. But he didn't fully appreciate the wreck of a man Noah had been. He couldn't. He didn't know the depths of his scars. If he did, he would thank Noah for walking away from the relationship.

So instead of explaining, Noah had returned to measuring and cutting the tiles that would go around the edge of the canteen floor. It was work that made his back hurt and his hands sore, but at least it kept him busy. He often stayed well after his crew left for the day because he didn't want to face the long and lonely hours at home.

There were no lunches with Sarah.

No walks in the park.

Nothing to look forward to but the next day and more work. Gideon tried to speak with him. Ezekiel tried to speak with him. Even Ada tried to talk to him about how much Sarah cared. But Noah didn't think that someone who cared could walk away from a relationship as Sarah had walked away from theirs. And more than that, he thought she'd done the right thing.

His parole officer was no help either. He simply reiterated what he'd said before.

You need to tell her.

Trust that she will understand.

Noah had no intention of confessing his past to Sarah. What had she said? *It's not like you killed anyone.* Maybe he had. He didn't know what the drugs he'd sold had done to the people who had taken them. He would carry that guilt—that burden—with him the rest of his life.

He trudged through the rest of that week and all of the next. He pretended to have a cold so he wouldn't have to go to the off-Sunday luncheon at the Yoder home. It was childish, but he told himself he was doing it to spare Sarah more embarrassment. He couldn't lie to himself, though. He knew full well that he was avoiding her because he was a coward.

The following day was a Monday, when the market was technically closed to visitors. The work crew was still remodeling the canteen. If Noah hadn't been so focused on his misery, he would have been pleased with what they had accomplished. The place was looking sharp, and the grand reopening was supposed to take place in just ten days.

His work crew had left for the day, and Noah was going over to the auction pens to help his *dat* unload three cows they planned to sell. His *dat* had hired an *Englisch* driver with a cattle trailer to transport them, and Noah was going to give his father a ride home. The cattle were off-loaded, and Noah thought they were done for the day.

But his father had wanted to check on the cows one last time. Assure himself that they were fine. One of the cows had always been a bit unpredictable. They'd even named her Chancy, because there was always a chance she'd decide to be obstinate. This day, she was simply unsettled and scared. When his *dat* stepped into the holding pen, the cows began moving about and Chancy moved sideways instead of away from his father.

Noah was standing outside the pen.

Calling to the cows.

Trying to lure them away from the corner where his *dat* stood. Noah was holding out a bucket of cattle cubes and rattling them, which always caused the cows to look up and trot toward him.

Two of the cows did just that, but not Chancy. Chancy jumped at the sound of the rattling cubes and jumped back and to the side. The animal slammed his father against the railing. One moment his *dat* was standing there, telling the cow to "get on, now." The next, he had fallen to the ground and Noah couldn't see him.

Either his father's cry of pain or Noah bounding over the fence finally got the cow moving, but his father didn't stand up. He lay there, groaning and clutching his right hip.

"*Dat*, are you okay?"

"Don't think I am, son." His face had gone whiter than a cloud on a summer day, and he was lying awkwardly on the ground.

"Leg?"

"Hip."

"We have to get you out of this pen."

"Don't think I'll be much help with that."

Gideon and Sarah both rushed into the fenced area. Sarah knelt in the dirt next to his *dat*. Gideon moved the cows out of the pen and into an adjacent one, then hurried back to where Noah's father still lay.

"He says it's his hip," Noah explained. "Broken, I think."

"Best not to move him then," Gideon cautioned. "We could damage it more, not to mention the pain would be terrible."

"It's bad enough as it is," his *dat* muttered, then tried to smile through his discomfort.

"I'll go call the ambulance." Sarah placed a hand on Noah's shoulder, squeezed it softly and then ran back to the office.

"What happened?" Gideon asked.

"Chancy pinned him."

"Not the cow's fault." Reuben's voice was quiet, matter of fact. "I should have given her more space."

Gideon offered a grim smile. "I suppose there's a reason you named her Chancy."

"Yup."

"You hanging in there, Reuben?"

"I am." Then in a softer, more frightened voice he said, "Don't leave me."

"We're not going anywhere, *Dat*." Noah had never seen his *dat* so vulnerable. He'd certainly never thought of him as old, but seeing him lying there on the ground, eyes closed, complexion a terrible white, Noah understood how much he loved his *dat*. How much he still needed him.

Gideon stayed with Noah as he sat in the dirt next to his father, afraid to move him, fervently praying he would be okay.

Sarah had gone to wait for the ambulance and direct them toward the animal pens. It seemed to take forever, but also seemed to happen in less time than it took to snap your fingers.

Two paramedics finally made their way into the animal pen, untroubled by the dirt and cow manure. The older man introduced himself as Grant, and the young woman with him was Vicki.

"Probably a broken hip," Grant confirmed. "Happens a couple of times a year. They'll fix you right up at the hospital, Mr. Beiler. We have top-notch surgeons in Goshen."

They quickly started an IV and moved him onto a stretcher.

"The pain meds should take effect almost immediately, Mr. Beiler." Vicki turned to Noah. "You can ride with us if you like."

It was then that Noah thought of his mother. "I need to go home. I need to take Beauty home and tell *mamm*..."

"I'll do that," Sarah said.

"And I'll contact Amos and the bishop," Gideon added. "I'll also call a driver to show up at your house. He'll take your *mamm* to the hospital."

"Give me a thirty-minute head start," Sarah said.

"You've got it."

Noah hesitated, realized he didn't have much choice, and murmured *thank you* as he jogged to catch up with the paramedics. His mind was split between what his father was going through and the look of sympathy in Sarah's eyes. She was a *gut* person. A compassionate person. How had he ever thought she could be anything else? How had he managed to doubt the one thing he should have been certain of—her kindness?

He rode in the back of the ambulance, siren blaring, lights flashing, his father drifting in and out of sleep from the pain medication they'd put in his IV. In the midst of all that, it occurred to him that Sarah and Gideon, Amos and Ezekiel, his work crew…they were all his friends. He might have ruined any chance of a romantic relationship with Sarah, but she was still his friend.

She hadn't hesitated to offer help when he had needed it.

He might never have a wife, might never be able to share all of himself, but he did at least have friends. That was something he was grateful for, something he had forgotten. It wasn't love, but it still mattered. And though it broke his heart anew to realize all he'd lost, he understood that friendship would have to be enough.

Sarah had always been good in a crisis. With four younger *schweschdern*, two of whom were very adept at getting into trouble, she'd had her share of minor medical emergencies.

Eunice had frequently managed to bust up her fingers, cut her hands or bruise her shoulders. She would be so focused on what she was doing that she'd forget to protect her body. Ada, on the other hand, was often simply clueless. One time she stepped into a hole and twisted her ankle because she'd been staring up at the budding trees. Another time, she sliced the pad of a finger while she was cutting up vegetables. That one had bled a lot. She'd explained that she was distracted by hummingbirds outside the window. Then there was the time she accidentally stirred up the beehive.

Bee stings.

That had been one of her first conversations with Noah.

She missed him. Missed talking with him every day. Missed laughing with him. She'd hoped that he might reconsider, that he might decide that he could trust her with his past. But that hadn't happened. One week had stretched into two, and her hope had turned into the sad realization that what had existed between them was over.

But the expression on his face as they'd waited by his father seemed to be more than gratitude. She thought there was something there. Something that could grow into a thing they could both cherish.

Or it might have been wishful thinking on her part.

She pulled into his driveway and forced her mind away from her own disappointments. Now wasn't the time for tossing around her relationship problems. Rachel would be in the kitchen preparing dinner, wondering why her son and husband weren't home yet.

Sarah directed Beauty right up to the front porch, set the brake and whispered, "I'll be back real quick, sweetheart." She hurried up the steps, knocked on the screen door, then opened it.

"Rachel? It's Sarah Yoder."

Rachel came out of the kitchen wiping her hands on a dish towel. Her face was flushed from working in the heat of the kitchen, but she smiled in greeting. "What a nice surprise. I didn't hear you knock."

"It's Reuben," Sarah rushed to explain. "He's been in an accident at the market. He's all right. But they think it's a broken hip."

"They?" Rachel blinked rapidly and her eyes darted to the front window and back again, as if she might see her husband outside, walking up the porch steps.

"The paramedics. Noah rode with him to the hospital in Goshen. Gideon has called a driver for you. He should be here in a few minutes."

Rachel sat down on the closest chair. "Oh. I didn't…that is, Reuben should be…" Her words faded away and her hands finally stopped worrying the dish towel.

"Are you okay?"

"*Ya.* I just need a minute." She pressed a trembling hand to her chest and pulled in a few deep breaths.

Sarah walked past her, into the kitchen, and fetched a glass of water. When Rachel had taken a few sips, the color came back to her face and her hands stopped shaking.

"He's okay, though?"

"*Ya.* The paramedics said he'll be fine after surgery."

"Right. Okay. And Noah is with him?"

"Noah stayed with him the entire time. The paramedics let him ride in the back of the ambulance with Reuben to the hospital."

"That's *gut*. He wasn't alone." She swiped at the tears running down her cheeks. "Reuben acts like a tough guy, but he told me once that he worries about being alone when he dies. His *dat* was alone. They didn't find him for a couple of hours. He was out working in the fields and had a heart attack."

"Rachel?"

"Ya?"

"Reuben isn't going to die, and he isn't alone."

"Right. I should..." Rachel glanced around. "I should gather up a few things."

"I'll unharness the mare."

She'd made it to the front door when Rachel asked, "You'll go with me?"

Sarah turned and studied this dear woman. There had been a time when she'd imagined Rachel being her mother-in-law. That dream had died, but perhaps they could still be friends. One could never have too many of those.

"Of course."

"Danki."

"Gem Gschehne."

Ten minutes later the horse had been released into the field, and they were sitting on the front porch waiting for the *Englisch* driver. Rachel had packed a bag. Sarah noticed a Bible and a ball of yarn peeking out of the top. When she saw those two things, she knew that Rachel was going to be fine. Noah's mom understood that there would be a lot of waiting over the next few days. She understood and planned accordingly.

"When I saw you standing in my sitting room, I thought something terrible had happened."

"A broken hip is no small thing."

"It isn't. But do you know what my first thought was?"

"Nein."

"*Not yet*. That's what I thought, Sarah. *Not yet*. It was a plea from the center of my heart that *Gotte* give us a little more time together."

Tears stung Sarah's eyes. She thought she understood what Rachel was describing, that abiding kind of love. Hadn't she seen her father sitting by her mother's bed in her last few hours? Hadn't the same plea for more time consumed him?

They both wiped at their faces, then Rachel looped her arm through Sarah's and clasped her hand.

"That old fool, I try to tell him to slow down, but he won't listen. He's a stubborn man."

"Aren't they all?" Sarah smiled as she said it, realizing that particular trait could describe her *dat*, her brothers-in-law, even Noah. It was one characteristic they all shared.

"You gave me a fright. I won't deny that. Reminded me of the time the police showed up, telling me that Noah had been arrested, that he was going to prison."

The birds had been singing.

A slight breeze had been cooling the July evening.

A barn cat had been rubbing up against Sarah's legs.

And at Rachel's words, all of those things stopped—abruptly and completely.

Sarah felt as if she'd been dropped into a very deep pool, as if she were seeing and hearing everything from a great distance. What had Rachel just said? Arrested? Prison? She finally found her voice. "Noah went to prison?"

Rachel's fingers went to her lips, but she seemed to quickly understand that what she'd said couldn't be taken back. "He never told you?"

"Nein."

"Those were difficult years. More difficult than this, if I'm being honest. And what point is there in being anything else?" She stood, paced down the porch steps as she looked toward the road, watching for the driver, eager to be with her husband. Finally, she sat down again, clasped one hand with the other, massaged her knuckles that were swollen with arthritis. "It's not my past to tell, Sarah. I honestly believe that my son has changed. That he's learned his lesson. He certainly paid his debt to society. Eight years is a long time to be locked in a cinderblock building."

"Eight years?"

"Longest eight years of my life."

"I had no idea."

"When they allowed him to come home, I vowed I'd never ask *Gotte* for anything again. As if *Gotte* can be bargained with. As if he didn't always have Noah in the palm of his hand."

His lost years.

Rachel had just explained Noah's lost years.

"We encouraged him to make a confession before the church, but Noah was afraid it would bring more criticism upon us." Rachel waved her hand as if pushing that idea away. "I only wanted him to have a clean, healthy start."

"Bishop Ezekiel knew?"

"*Ya*. Of course he did. Ezekiel encouraged him the entire time he was in prison. And when Noah returned home, he didn't insist on a confession because Noah wasn't a member of the church when those things happened."

Sarah felt as if she couldn't swallow. She pushed the next question out with great effort. "And my *dat*?"

Rachel turned and studied her, reached for Sarah's hands and squeezed them. "A condition of his parole is that his employer know his history. We will always be grateful to Amos for taking a chance on Noah. And the fact that he didn't share Noah's history with you? Well, that speaks to what a *gut* man your father is."

Sarah's mind was reeling.

Her bishop had known.

Her father had known.

Rachel and Reuben and Amos and Ezekiel. They had been the only four to understand all that Noah was trying to overcome. Other than that very small group, Noah had been carrying this burden alone since the day he'd returned to Shipshe? She'd thought that he didn't know about the gossip, but of course he'd known. He'd known and ignored it because…what was it Rachel had said? *Noah was afraid it would bring more criticism upon us.*

She knew that was true—unfair but true. When a child strayed from how they were raised, the fault was placed squarely at the feet of the parents. Somehow that made everyone else feel better, safer. People convinced themselves that it couldn't happen to them because they'd done everything right raising their children.

No one did everything right.

And Noah's past choices had been just that—his choices.

"How is it that I never heard? What I mean is, how do you keep something like that a secret?"

"I suppose it helped that his arrest and incarceration were both in Illinois. He'd lived there for some time...before."

Suddenly it all made sense to Sarah. Like pieces of a jigsaw puzzle falling into place, all of the answers to the questions she'd puzzled over fell into her lap.

Noah's inability or unwillingness to talk about his past.

His wisdom that seemed to belong to a much older man.

Stuart and George.

The missing ten years.

Just then, an *Englisch* car pulled into the drive. Before she could respond in any way to what Rachel had said, they were in the car, driving to the hospital in Goshen. She realized as they fell into a prayerful silence in the backseat of the automobile that Rachel wasn't the person she needed to talk to.

She needed to speak with Noah.

She needed to apologize.

And more than anything, she needed to tell him that his past didn't matter to her.

She hoped that his feelings for her hadn't changed. She hoped that she wasn't too late.

Chapter Eleven

The scene in the waiting room might have looked odd to anyone unfamiliar with Amish ways. To Sarah, it looked perfectly normal. The chairs were already beginning to fill up with friends, neighbors and her family. Her relationship with Noah might be over, or it might merely be on pause, but her family had grown quite close to his. They were determined to show up and support Reuben and Rachel in their hour of need.

Gideon and Becca were there. "We dropped Mary off with Bethany. She and Aaron wanted to be here, but they offered to keep the little ones. And Eunice stayed home to take care of morning chores."

Ada was there with her husband Ethan. "Ethan wanted to come without me, but I told him to hold his giddy-up."

"Hold his horses?"

"No way he was coming without me. Rachel and Reuben and Noah are like part of the family. In spite of, well, you know..." Her voice trailed off and her vast quantity of misquotes seemed to fail her, so she pulled Sarah into a hug.

Ezekiel was there, reminding them to pray, offering to fetch coffee, even telling funny stories about Rachel and Reuben's wedding day.

"I was a young bishop back them." His expression took on a distant look, as if he were seeing into the past. "I hadn't done a lot of weddings, and suddenly I forgot what I was supposed to say. Reuben and Rachel had agreed to be loyal and care for each other during adversity and affliction—"

"And sickness." Rachel's voice was soft. Her gaze also pinned on some long-ago day, her heart caught up in the memory.

"And sickness," Ezekiel agreed. "I remember I tucked my Bible under my arm, covered their hands with my own."

He held out his hand, now speckled with age spots. "Suddenly, I couldn't think of a thing to say."

"Reuben leaned toward Ezekiel and whispered that he was to give us his blessing." Rachel chuckled and an expression of love and happiness and gratitude covered her face.

"Ha! Which is exactly what I did." Ezekiel dabbed at his eyes, unashamed that remembering that long-ago moment had touched his heart. He allowed his gaze to brush over Rachel, Amos, Gideon and Becca, Ada and Ethan. "As I have with each of you. I wished you the blessing and mercy of *Gotte*. It has been my great privilege to be your bishop all these years. I don't thank you often enough."

The moment had turned quite serious. Sarah was trying mightily not to look at Noah, but when she did, when her gaze inadvertently drifted up and over to him, she saw that he was watching her. Something in her heart lifted then. Hope, perhaps.

A nurse came out to the waiting room. "I wanted to update you and let you know that Mr. Beiler is in surgery now."

"And he's okay?" Rachel popped to her feet and stood clasping her hands. "He's doing well?"

"His stats are all perfect. I'll come out and update you every hour or so. The surgery usually takes about three hours to complete."

Sarah's gaze flew to the clock on the wall. Two minutes after eleven. It was going to be a very long night. She wanted to talk to Noah. She wanted to confess to him that she knew about his past and that it didn't matter. She wanted to tell him that she loved him.

But she understood that now wasn't the time.

She would wait to share those things that weighed so heavily on her heart. But she couldn't wait another moment to show him some little kindness. She stood, wondered if everyone was watching her, and walked over to where he was sitting.

"Would you like to take a walk?"

He looked up from the magazine he'd been flipping through. He stared at her as if he didn't understand what she'd asked.

She stumbled on. "Maybe we could find something to eat? There are some very good vending machines down the hall. That's not true. I don't know why I said it. I'm exaggerating. The food in those machines is truly terrible, but it's something."

Surprise and maybe relief—she hoped it was relief—changed his expression, softened his gaze, caused a very small smile to tug at the corners of his lips.

"*Ya.* I'd like that."

They walked down the hall, past the vending machines, made a left and walked down the next hall. The hospital corridors formed a kind of square. Each time they passed the waiting room they slowed and peered over to Rachel and Ezekiel and Amos. Each time they could tell that no news had been received. So they'd make another circuit.

"Feels better to be moving," Noah admitted. "Thought I was going to jump out of my suspenders sitting there and waiting."

"Waiting is always hard. The night that Becca

and Bethany had their babies, I won't forget it even if I live to be one hundred and one."

Noah nodded in agreement. "Isn't it odd how each day feels important—all the minor things like getting stuck behind an *Englisch* tractor on the road..."

"Or my nieces spilling a glass of milk."

"Or an order being shipped wrong."

They both laughed at that. The week before they'd received a box of baby mobiles featuring ponies. What they had ordered was a box of condiment holders in the shape of a horse and buggy for the canteen.

"Those things feel important when you're going through them," Sarah said. "But then time passes."

"And what stands out in your memory—in your heart—is your *dat* being crushed by a cow or friends showing up at the hospital."

"Or your parents' wedding vows."

"I haven't thanked you for taking the horse and buggy home. For staying with my *mamm*. For riding here with her. I'm sure you were a great comfort to her."

"She's a special woman. It was amazing how quickly she recovered from the shock."

"Yup. Not a lot rattles Rachel Beiler."

They had stopped at a window that looked out over the parking area. Low outside lighting revealed enough of the scene that she could make out the limbs of the trees being stirred by the wind. She felt like that. Like a limb that had been stirred back to life. All from a confession that slipped from Rachel's lips.

"I'm sorry, Noah."

He turned to look at her, surprise coloring his features.

She wanted to tell him everything then, but she knew it wasn't the right time. She could wait. She would wait. Noah was worth waiting for. So instead of saying what was weighing so mightily on her heart, she said, "I'm sorry about your *dat*." And then she stood on tiptoe and kissed his cheek.

He looked surprised.

He looked happy.

"We should get back," he said huskily.

"Right."

Had she overstepped? But then he reached for her hand, clasped it in his, and Sarah felt such a rush of relief that she very nearly burst into tears. She didn't. This night wasn't about her. It was about family, friends and being a good neighbor.

Once Reuben's surgery was over and he was resting comfortably in his room, she would have a heart-to-heart talk with the man walking beside her. Until then, it was enough that the great gulf between them had been bridged.

That evening was one that Noah would remember for the rest of his life. His family had always been small—just the three of them. Even when he was a child, he'd felt the difference between their family and others. He'd felt the need to apologize for not having a buggy full of siblings. Of course, by the time he was a teenager, it had seemed normal. But he'd always felt a bit isolated. A bit out of step with the rest of the community. Perhaps that was typical for a teenager, or maybe it was that he hadn't yet processed how and why his family was different.

Then he'd moved to Illinois.

Fallen in with the wrong crowd.

Made mistake after mistake after mistake.

He didn't know what his parents' lives were like after he was sentenced to ten years in the Illinois State Prison system. He suspected that they kept to themselves. It would have been easier to turn down social invitations rather than answer well-meaning questions.

He imagined their life had been lonely.

That their circle of friends had grown even smaller than before.

The evening in the hospital had reminded Noah that they weren't alone, and he could tell that his parents were acutely aware of it too. They were a part of a large, caring community. Over the next week, neighbors brought casseroles, took care of their horses and livestock, helped with the tending of the crops. Noah couldn't have possibly done it all on his own, and he didn't have to. Neither he or his *mamm* or his *dat* even had to ask. Those things were simply taken care of in the way that their community had always taken care of one another.

Noah realized he had focused too much on the problems with a small community—everyone knowing everyone else's business, people's natural curiosity, even the occasional rude or callous remark. He'd let those small things become inexplicably large. They weren't, though. They were all results of people being people.

Yet, they still had the inclination to be kind.

They possessed a generous nature.

And maybe for the first time in his life, he understood what it meant for someone to be the hands and feet of Christ to someone else. He'd heard that particular topic preached on more times than he could count. But until you were the recipient of such kindness, he didn't think you could fully understand it.

The accident with Chancy the cow had occurred on Monday afternoon.

By Tuesday morning, his *dat* was in his hospital room and resting comfortably, vowing that a cow would never get the better of him again.

The doctors kept him two additional nights. Noah's *mamm* stayed with him, of course. Noah went home to take care of chores, only to find they were already done. He heated up a serving of chicken casserole that had been left in the refrigerator, warmed two slices of the freshly baked bread that had been left on the counter, and took a piece of homemade apple pie to the front porch swing with a cup of coffee.

He sat there, rocking, enjoying the food and realizing that he had much to be grateful for. He'd been so focused on the past that he hadn't been able to see what was right in front of him. The crops growing in the field. The mares grazing next to the barn. The satisfaction of being home.

While Noah was going back and forth between the farm and the hospital, bringing whatever his parents needed, and being present for doctors' rounds, men from his church had built a ramp to access the porch for his *dat*.

It wasn't there Tuesday morning when he left.

When he arrived back at the farm Tuesday night, it was completed.

"Many hands make for a light task," Ezekiel had said when Noah asked him about it.

"I don't know how we'll ever repay them."

"You're not supposed to." Ezekiel had tapped his cane against the hospital linoleum. "You're supposed to do the same when someone else needs your help."

"I will."

"I am sure that you will, Noah."

His *dat* came home on Wednesday—using a walker, though the doctors had assured him that would only be necessary for a few weeks. Thursday was the first day that Noah made it back to work at the market. He found that his crew had finished painting the walls of the canteen and affixed the new baseboards. They'd also meticulously cleaned up any spots of paint on the new tile. The area looked good, as if it had been remodeled by professionals.

All that was left to do was install artwork on the walls, unbox the new tables and chairs and set out the decorative containers along the serving line and on each table. Then they'd do a final check of the large room to be sure that everything was as it should be.

"I was worried we might have to push back our grand opening," Noah admitted.

"Not going to happen," Andrew said.

"My grandmother is coming," Stanley said with a grin. "We can't change the date."

Deborah rubbed at a splotch of paint on her palm. "We put flyers out all over town. This is happening next Wednesday."

They all told him that it was good to have him back, and Noah realized they meant it. They'd become a solid work crew. They looked out for one another.

Only Sarah had been silent as he'd met with the team. He hadn't allowed himself to think about her. Every time he wanted to dwell on the kiss she'd given his cheek that night in the hospital, he pushed the memory away. He didn't know what it meant. He didn't know what had changed. He didn't know what to say or do or feel. Now it was only the two of them in the canteen, and still she didn't speak.

"Is everything okay?" he asked.

"*Ya*. Sure. Glad to hear your *dat* is home."

"He is thrilled to be out of the hospital. Another night of being woken by nurses every couple of hours might have sent him over the edge." He laughed, then added, "Now my *mamm* is in charge of his care. He won't get away with a thing. His first physical therapy appointment is tomorrow."

"That's really *gut* to hear, Noah." She smiled and blushed slightly, then added, "I like your parents."

"They like you." He wanted to add more to that statement, which seemed woefully inadequate. He wasn't sure now was the best time to get into the questions he had about their relationship. Did they even have a relationship?

He needn't have worried about how to broach the subject.

"I was hoping to speak with you," Sarah said, fidgeting with her *kapp* strings, looking everywhere but directly at him. "If you have a few minutes."

"*Ya*. Of course I do."

"Maybe we could…maybe take a walk?"

"I'd like that."

They stepped out into a hot July day. Noah didn't care about the temperature. He was happy to be outside, to be away from the sterile environment of the hospital. He'd be happy if he didn't have to ride in an *Englisch* car again for the next year. His parents' old buggy and the mare Beauty suited him just fine.

They walked toward the back of the market, and stopped at the picnic tables situated next to the small creek, beneath the shade of a stand of Eastern cottonwoods. Sarah sat on one of the benches, so he sat beside her. Then she popped up and paced in front of him, then sat again.

"What's wrong?" he asked.

"Nothing. Well, that is to say, nothing that can't be fixed with a little frank discussion. I hope. And I know you're tired. I'll try to keep it short."

"I'm right here, Sarah. Talk to me."

"Okay."

When she still didn't speak, he added, "I've never known you to be tongue-tied."

She stood again. Resumed her pacing. "Ada would probably say that the canary has caught my tongue."

He didn't answer. He didn't know what else to say to her, but it was plain that she was agitated. If he could help in any way, he would. He didn't know how though, so he waited.

Finally, Sarah said, "When your *dat* was hurt, I went to your *mamm*'s."

"Right. You told her what had happened, and then you waited with her. You even rode to the hospital with her. *Danki*."

She nodded, but plainly her mind was wrestling with something else. Noah's stomach flipped, wondering what this was actually about. Some well-honed instinct told him that everything was about to change—again.

"As we waited for the driver, your *mamm* admitted that I'd given her quite a fright. She said that it reminded her of another time."

Now she stopped in front of him, and Noah felt a great and terrible worry lodge in his throat.

"She said it reminded her of the time that the police had come, telling her you'd been arrested and that you were going to prison."

And with those words, a blanket of shame covered Noah.

He leaned forward, elbows on his knees, hands covering his face. So, this was why Sarah had been so kind to him at the hospital. Why she'd offered her friendship again. Friendship, nothing else. He'd foolishly hoped that perhaps she'd decided to forget the situation in Grand Rapids. But Sarah wasn't that kind of person. She wouldn't settle for anything less than complete honesty, and she shouldn't have to.

Now she stood in front of him—waiting.

She waited, and he pulled himself together.

He sat up straighter, squared his shoulders and

finally met her gaze. "I'm sorry. I should have told you. My parents advised me to. Bishop Ezekiel advised me to. Even my parole officer advised me to."

"You have a parole officer?"

"*Ya*, I do. Sit with me, Sarah. I'll answer any of your questions, and trust me—I understand why you don't want to have a relationship with me."

"That isn't true."

"What?"

"Your past is just that, Noah. It's your past. I still care about you."

"Okay. I know you think you do, but when you hear the details—"

"I'll feel the same. But I still want to understand. I want to know what you've been through."

She finally walked around the table and sat across from him, no longer pacing, no longer flustered. "And if you'd rather wait to have this conversation, that's okay too."

"*Nein*. I've already waited long enough." He swung his legs around so that they were facing each other.

On a normal summer afternoon, were they a normal couple, they'd be sharing a meal, talking about their day, discussing their future. But this wasn't that. He stared at his hands, then at the picnic table where several couples *in lieb* had carved their initials within a heart. He wondered if that might have been the two of them—if things were different.

The past was past, though.

He couldn't change it, no matter how much he longed to.

"When I was a *youngie*, I started hanging out with the wrong crowd."

"Amish?"

"And *Englisch*. I won't blame them. I made my own decisions. After a few months of our parents harassing us, we decided to go to the city."

"The city?"

"Chicago." He laughed, but even he could hear there was no humor in it. "We thought all of the answers were in Chicago. That's where I started selling, and I was already using heavily."

"Marijuana?"

"At first, *ya*. Then Oxy, Ritalin, Adderall—pretty much anything that would give me a high."

He paused, giving her time to absorb what he'd shared.

Her question, when it came, surprised him.

"Do you miss it? That feeling of being…high?"

"I do not."

She nodded as if she believed him. "And you were caught?"

"*Ya*. They have a three-strike law in Illinois. It means if you're convicted in three separate instances, they can be quite strict with the sentencing. I was given ten years, and honestly that was lenient. Once I was inside, I knew plenty of men who received much longer sentences."

"For using drugs?"

"Using and selling."

"Right." Sarah reached for his hands, ran her fingers over the back of his. "Ten years. Your lost ten years. You spent them all in prison."

"I spent eight and a half in prison. The first year and a half I spent on the street. I won't sugarcoat it, Sarah. I was homeless and desperate. You wouldn't have recognized the person I was then. When I was released early for good behavior, my parents paid the lawyer to take the terms of my parole before the judge and ask for me to be paroled to Indiana. So I could come home."

"Otherwise you would have had to stay in Illinois?"

"Ya."

"Your poor parents."

"Ya."

She was still holding his hands, and he took that as a good sign. Looking up, she asked, "Stuart and George..."

"Stuart was my cellmate for a while. I'd never met George before that night in Grand Rapids."

"What were the terms of your parole? Am I saying that correctly?"

"Yes. My terms included having gainful employment, checking in regularly with my parole officer and submitting to random drug tests—all of which I've passed."

"I'm sure you have."

"You are?"

"Yes, Noah. It's plain that you've put those days behind you."

He nodded, but tears were blurring his vision and he couldn't find his voice. It was his turn to stand, pace away from the table and back again. "I had to receive special permission from my parole officer to even go to Grand Rapids. My life—it will never completely be my own now. I've come to terms with that. At least I think I have."

Noah hesitated, then he asked, "Do you remember when I told you about my dog?"

"Libby?"

"Right. I wasn't here when she passed. I wasn't here for my *dat*'s fiftieth birthday or my *mamm*'s. I missed so many things, and I can't ever have those years back."

"That must have been very hard."

Hard didn't begin to describe his wretchedness, his remorse. "Can we walk?"

"Sure. *Ya*."

Noah wanted to reach for her hand, but he didn't trust himself yet. He wasn't quite done baring his soul.

"Do you remember when you came to me after the Grand Rapids trip?"

"I do."

"You wanted to know about my lost years. You said it wasn't like I had killed anyone."

"I remember."

"But what if I did kill someone, Sarah?" Misery flooded his soul as he voiced his worst fear. This was the thing, more than any other, that woke him in the middle of the night. This was the thing that he simply could not forgive himself for. How could he? "What if someone I sold drugs to died? How am I supposed to live with that?"

They'd been walking toward the creek, but Sarah reached out, snagged his arm, pulled him to a stop. When he looked at her, he was surprised to see tears slipping down her cheeks. He reached forward, thumbed them away, regretted having brought so much pain into her life.

"I don't know the answer to that. Whoever you sold drugs to made the decision to use those substances. If you hadn't sold to them, someone else would have." She pressed her fingertips to his lips when he tried to argue. "I'm not excusing what you did, Noah. It was wrong. You know it was wrong, and you served your sentence. You don't have to carry that burden any longer."

"Okay." He swiped at his eyes with the back of his hand. "Okay. Maybe I can eventually get to the place where I accept that, where I believe what you're saying. But—"

"But what?"

"But you deserve better, Sarah. You shouldn't

waste your time, waste your affection, on someone like me."

"You don't get to decide that, Noah." She stepped closer, stepped into the circle of his arms. "You don't get to decide who I care about. That's my decision, and I care about you."

He pulled her closer then.

Let himself hold her.

Let himself believe.

Chapter Twelve

Sarah had lived through several watershed moments in her life. Her *mamm*'s death. Learning her *dat* had heart disease. The birth of her nieces. All of those things had fundamentally changed who she was and how she viewed her life.

And now she and Noah had finally been completely honest with each other. It was literally like the difference between night and day, between darkness and light. Her doubts about his feelings for her faded away. She knew he cared. He showed her in a dozen small ways. If she had a question about his past, she asked him. Each time he nodded as if he could understand why she'd want to know, and he answered as honestly as he could.

What was the food like in prison? Mostly terrible.

Had his family visited him? His *mamm* had come twice a year, his *dat* had only been able to get away four times in the entire eight years. Reuben had carried the bulk of the farm responsibilities. He'd continued shouldering the burden of all the planting, harvesting, home repairs and animal care. At the time when his *dat* had thought he'd be slowing down and his son would be taking the reins, the exact opposite happened. He'd had to adjust. They'd all had to adjust.

Had Bishop Ezekiel visited? No, but he'd faithfully written letters every week.

Sometimes Noah offered up random bits of information, when they were eating lunch together or taking walks or riding in the buggy.

He'd earned his GED while incarcerated.

At first he'd rejected his faith. Later, he'd clung to it.

He'd learned to basket weave.

"Basket weaving?" Sarah had tried to keep a straight face, but she couldn't help bursting into laughter at Noah's serious expression.

"It's a very calming hobby." Then he had squinted at her and said in a low voice. "What are you laughing about, woman? A man can enjoy basket weaving. I'll have you know I was quite *gut* at it."

"I'm sorry." She put a hand to her side. "I'm so sorry. I'm just trying to picture you…basket weaving."

"Play your cards right, and you might receive one of my baskets for Christmas."

They'd both laughed then. What a sweet thing

it was to share a memory and find the light inside of it.

The weekend following their talk had been a church weekend. They'd sat together at lunch, sat with all of Sarah's *schweschdern* and their families. They'd taken a walk, holding hands. They'd once again stepped into the public eye with their relationship.

The following Wednesday was the grand reopening of the canteen at the market. Amos stood next to the canteen's door, shaking hands and greeting people. Sarah waited near the walkway, directing folks to the newly remodeled facility.

The head of the local chamber of commerce approached her and introduced himself. "You're one of Amos's daughters."

"Yes, I'm Sarah. I'm the oldest."

"Your father has done a wonderful job here."

"Actually, Noah Beiler was in charge of the work," Sarah said, pointing him out to the chamber president.

"Sounds like a young man I should meet."

Sarah was so happy for Noah in that moment. Each day she was grateful for the fact that he was in her life and that he was successful in his job at the market, but as he stood there answering questions and explaining the details of the project, she realized just how far he had come. It wasn't only that he wasn't using drugs anymore, or that he'd positioned himself on the right side of the law.

Those were important things for sure. But it was that he was confident in who he was as a person. He'd found a job that he enjoyed, excelled at and found satisfaction in. He'd embraced the life he had here, in his hometown.

That had taken courage.

It had taken resolve.

A reporter and photographer from the local paper were also there. Although Amish weren't big fans of having their pictures taken, they'd formed a line—all of the men and women who worked in the canteen, as well as Noah's work crew. Amos had stood on one end. Noah had stood on the other. They'd stood with their backs to the camera, a red ribbon that was about to be cut in front of them.

They all laughed over the article, which came out the next day. The headline read, "A Plain and Simple Reopening."

Amos's secretary, Miranda, framed a copy of the article and Noah put it on the wall in the entryway to the canteen. Sarah sat at her kitchen table reading over the article and again marveling at how far Noah had come.

Anyone else would look at the photo and see the backs of men in suspenders, and the backs of women in long dresses and *kapps*. Sarah looked at it and saw her friends, her coworkers, her *dat* and the man that she was falling in love with. She ran her fingers over the picture, said a silent prayer of thanks, then folded it and put it between the pages of her journal.

On the following Sunday, the last in July, Sarah planned a special luncheon. It was an off-Sunday, and she wanted to have private time with Noah's family, her family, and the bishop. The meal had been Sarah's idea, but Noah had suggested that he share his past with everyone at once.

"You don't have to do that."

"I want to do it."

"Okay. Then we'll do it." She couldn't help grinning broadly.

"Happy?"

"I am." She threw her arms around him, then kissed him on the cheek.

"Whoa. What's that for?"

"Just because you're you."

"Who else would I be?" And then his voice had turned husky, and he'd kissed her softly, sweetly.

Sarah had always approached things slowly, had always been somewhat serious and cautious. As the oldest *schweschder*, she'd taken her role as substitute *mamm* seriously. She'd tried to make sure that no one got hurt, that no one's heart was broken, that her *schweschdern* were safe. That she was safe. With Noah, she was finally allowing herself to step out of that role and into her own life. She allowed herself to feel and appreciate the joy of being in love, of dreaming of their future and of waking each day eager to see what would happen next.

And yet, she understood that this revelation of his past would be a serious moment too. It was a big step forward…and a step away from shame and secrecy.

She woke that Sunday morning to the sound of a steady rain beating against the roof. Even that couldn't dampen her grateful mood. Rain was *gut* and necessary. The cooler temperature was a blessing. They'd set up the luncheon in the open area of the barn and leave the double doors flung open to let in fresh air and the sun's muted light.

Noah waited until the meal was over and the children were growing drowsy. Then everyone settled in rocking chairs and on top of overturned crates and even on hay bales. The dessert table held chocolate cake, cherry pie, fresh strawberries and peanut butter cookies. They would taste of those *wunderbaar* things after the discussion.

"If they don't all storm out," Noah whispered as they waited for everyone to settle.

"My family would never do that, plus your parents and my *dat* already know."

Sarah and Noah stood together in front of those assembled.

"We wanted a chance to talk to you—all of you—at the same time." Sarah turned and smiled at Noah, felt a tenderness swell in her heart that was nearly overwhelming. "Noah has some things to share, and then if you have any questions...absolutely any questions at all, he'll try to answer them. Or if you have questions for me. We just... we wanted you to hear these things from us first, not from the grapevine."

"If you're talking about the gossip vine, no thank you," Ada proclaimed. "Those grapes are sour."

"Indeed they are," Noah said.

Then he started at the beginning. He explained about experimenting with drugs, his worsening addiction, his move to Chicago, living on the streets and being arrested, selling to other users, being arrested again. Not learning his lesson. Falling into despondency. Turning his back on his faith and his family and his community. Being arrested a third time and sentenced to ten years in the Illinois State Prison. Serving eight and a half. Coming home. Being given a second chance by Amos.

It was a lot of information that he managed to share in less time than it had taken Sarah to mix together the chocolate cake batter. All eyes were focused on him. And when Sarah looked at her family, before anyone said a single word, she understood that their expressions reflected surprise but also love and compassion.

"I have a question," Ada said. "And I'm being serious, so you all can stop rolling your eyes. I want to know why folks call someone who is released from prison, someone who has served their time and paid their debt, why do they call that person a *jail canary*."

If there was any tension in the group, it went away with those words. They all smiled, murmured "*gut question*," and waited to see how Noah would answer that.

Finally, he said, "Maybe some people call us a *jail canary*. I've never heard that particular expression. I've heard *jailbird*, and I think it's because when you're in prison, when you're locked in a cell, one of the things you long for is the simplicity of seeing a bird fly across the sky."

Some of the questions were more serious.

How long would he be on parole? Five more years.

Was he limited in what he could do or where he could go? Yes. Any travels out of the state had to be approved by his parole officer. He could not own a gun or hunting rifle. He couldn't work in education or healthcare. He couldn't vote until the end of his parole.

Did he ever hear from any of the friends he made while incarcerated? No. He hadn't. Other than running into an old cellmate in Grand Rapids. Everyone's eyes darted to Sarah when he said that.

"Ya." Noah stared at the ground, then looked up, a smile tugging at the corner of his lips. "Needless to say, Sarah had a few questions, which I wasn't ready to answer at the time."

"While you were in prison, were you able to attend church?" Gideon asked and shook his head. "I can't imagine eight years without learning or worshipping together."

"We did. Of course, it wasn't like our services. There weren't many other Amish men incarcerated where I was. But we had preachers who visited and gave a Bible study. One week it would be a Baptist minister, another week it would be a Catholic priest."

"And did it help? Even though it was different?"

"It did. Maybe because they realized they were addressing a tough audience, they kept their sermons simple and interesting. Mostly they reminded us of God's mercy and grace."

"I'll bet the singing wasn't as *gut* as ours," Ada said.

"It wasn't, Ada. But some of the hymns were the same. And the chairs were more comfortable than our benches."

That elicited more laughter from everyone.

A few questions were for Reuben and Rachel, who seemed relieved to finally be able to share their part of the story. Up to that point, they'd only discussed it with Ezekiel. It seemed to Sarah that now they could see the benefits of widening their circle, letting others in and sharing their burden.

"I didn't know how to explain what had happened," Rachel admitted. "Especially at first, I was afraid I'd break into tears if I talked about it at all. So, I'd simply say that Noah was away. People seemed to accept that. Over the years, it became a habit to simply not speak of it."

"I can tell you that ten years sounded like a long time." Reuben reached for his wife's hand. "Noah began writing to us again, and it was *wunderbaar* to hear from him. But we had no idea what kind of treatment he was receiving there. No idea what his life was like."

"And no one to ask about it. No way to know if the things we were feeling were normal."

"We'd forgotten how it felt to have real friends," Reuben said.

Rebecca wiped her eyes, then added, "You all have helped us to see just how important friends are."

When they'd explored Noah's history thoroughly and completely, Ezekiel stood and said he'd like to offer a blessing.

It was for far more than the dessert they were about to eat.

It was a blessing on Noah's life.

On his family's path forward.

On his relationship with Sarah.

And on the friendships deepened that day between them all.

Little Mary and Lydia asked for one of *Aenti* Sarah's cookies. Soon they were all filling their plates, pouring glasses of water and milk and tea.

They enjoyed the desserts, spoke of the following week and weather forecasts and fall plans.

Over the course of the next hour, as the little group broke up, Sarah stood beside Noah as each person in her family approached them. They promised to pray for his continued recovery. Told him that it had taken guts to share as he had. Insisted that both he and Sarah promise to say something if they needed anything at all. Ada and Ethan, Bethany and Aaron, Becca and Gideon, Sarah's father and Eunice, Noah's parents, Ezekiel—everyone offered their help and prayers.

Becca pulled Sarah into a hug and said, "I'm so happy for you, sis. Happy for you both."

For Sarah it felt as if she was receiving the blessing of every single person who mattered to her. It felt as if she and Noah weren't alone in this, and they weren't. They had a large and faithful group standing behind them.

When the bishop and Noah and his parents had left, when her *schweschdern* had helped to clean up the dishes and then gone to their own homes, Sarah sat on the front porch and stared out across the only place she'd ever lived. She looked out through the rain that continued to fall—let her gaze take in the barn, the fields, the homes beyond.

"Today was a *gut* day," her *dat* said, lowering himself into the chair next to her.

"It was." She studied him for a moment, then said, "You knew all along."

"I knew some of it. Per the terms of Noah's parole, he had to make his employer aware of his sentencing."

"But you never said a word."

She thought he wouldn't answer. He smiled, set the chair in motion, drummed his fingers against the arm of the old hackberry rocker. Finally, he shrugged slightly. "Wasn't my story to tell."

Which seemed to sum it up nicely.

Her father respected Noah. Respected his privacy and his efforts to build a new life.

Sarah stood, walked over to her *dat*, and kissed him on the top of the head, which caused him to laugh. Then she went inside and prepared for bed. She really didn't know where her relationship with Noah would go from here, what would happen next, or even what they wanted to happen next. But she knew that she and Noah would figure out all of those things together.

A younger Noah would have assumed there would be nothing but smooth sailing ahead for him, his family and Sarah. The older, wiser, more experienced Noah understood that probably wouldn't be the case. Trouble often popped up when you were least expecting it. Trials were a part of life.

The following week, his crew began working

on a remodeled entry for the market. It would include repainting the fencing, installing new flower beds and shrubs, ordering and installing new signage, adding park benches, water stations, and a new information stand. It was their largest, most in-depth project to date, and Noah was ready to take it on.

His crew was eager to get to work.

Life was good. Not perfect, but good.

He occasionally heard under-the-breath comments about his past from folks both at the market and at church. He would have confronted the person, but he could never make out exactly who had said what.

Twice he found notes in his work locker. One said, "We don't want people like you here." The other was more specific. "Drug dealers belong in jail."

He shared both of the notes with Amos, who advised that he ignore them. He also told Sarah, whose advice was similar to her father's.

But those were small things, and Noah had learned to have a strong outer shell. He wasn't hurt by the rude comments or notes. He was puzzled. What did they hope to gain? Did they think he would turn tail and run away?

He didn't do either of those things.

Instead, he began to court Sarah in earnest.

He took her to dinner, on long drives, on walks through the park, even on kayak trips. Their feelings for each other grew, and he began to entertain notions of marrying her. Not soon, of course. He needed to save some money, build her a proper house, perhaps even purchase their own land—though he knew his parents hoped he would stay on the family farm.

Would Sarah want that?

It was too soon to ask.

One Saturday they had a driver take them to an art festival in downtown Goshen. They walked through the booths, browsed the art gallery and enjoyed dinner at a restaurant with outdoor seating.

It was while they were there, enjoying burgers and fries and shakes, that he noticed the homeless man hanging around the patrons waiting for a table. Someone who worked for the restaurant went out and tried to shoo him off. It didn't work. Finally the police were called. An officer spoke with the man, who might have been thirty or sixty—it was difficult to tell beneath the grime. The man shuffled off, though he stopped several yards down, still eyeing the restaurant.

And Noah understood in that moment that his past, his time on the streets and in prison, had changed him. He wasn't the person he'd been before, or the person he would have grown into if he hadn't made those mistakes. He was different from most of the people in his community. From most of the people in this restaurant.

"Do you mind if I... I need to do something."

"*Ya*. Sure." Sarah looked surprised, but not alarmed.

He walked over to their waitress, asked for a to-go container, then thanked her. Hurrying back to their table, he packed half of his burger and a good portion of the fries into the to-go box.

"Take my shake," Sarah said.

"You're sure?"

"Yes. We'll share yours."

Noah squeezed her hand, fetched a to-go cup, then hurried out onto the sidewalk with the food. The guy he'd been watching hadn't moved. When Noah approached him, he startled and became instantly defensive.

"I'm not causing trouble."

"Didn't say you were." Noah stopped a good three feet from the guy. "Thought you could use a meal."

"Why do you say that?"

"Because you look hungry." Noah held out the offering.

He worried for a moment that the man would refuse, that some deep-seated, misplaced sense of pride would win. Instead, he ducked his head and said, "Yeah. I guess I am."

When he accepted the food, Noah noticed his hand shaking.

"My name's Noah."

"Gus." He'd opened the box and began wolfing down the food.

"My girlfriend and I were eating at the restaurant."

"Good for you."

"Is there somewhere we can take you?"

Now the man's expression twisted into a sardonic grin. "In your horse and buggy?"

"Actually, we hired a driver. We'll catch another Uber to take us back home. We live over in Shipshe. It wouldn't be a hardship to share the ride with you."

Gus had devoured all the food. Now he carefully placed the to-go box and cup in a trash bin.

"What do you say? You must have family or friends. Someone who would be relieved to see you."

"Nope."

"Getting clean is hard, but it's worth it."

"What would you know about that?"

"Everything," Noah said.

Gus looked at him then, really looked at him. Noah wondered what he saw. Sure, an Amish guy wearing plain trousers and a button-up shirt, suspenders, hat. But Gus seemed to peer deeper, as if he could see into Noah's soul. As if he could see who Noah had once been.

"Thanks for the food, man." And then he was gone, shuffling off into the crowd. The carbs would hit his system soon, and he'd be looking for a place to sleep it off. Noah remembered that feeling well. He remembered all of it—the hunger, the embarrassment, the constant worry.

Noah made his way back to the restaurant and Sarah and his life. After they'd paid for their meal, they decided to walk off the food before hailing one of the Uber drivers that waited on the streets. It was one of the unique aspects of Amish communities that they had Uber drivers waiting about, but the drivers realized that Amish didn't have phones and so had learned where to queue up in order to make it easier for them to use the service.

"That was very kind of you," Sarah said.

"You're the one who gave up your shake." He bumped his shoulder against hers. "That was kind of you."

"He took the food?"

"He did."

"Did you try to talk to him?"

"I tried." He glanced at her, reached for her hand, let the anxiety and feelings of loss wash over and out of him.

They stopped and listened to a band.

He purchased a small bundle of flowers from one of the street vendors and handed them to Sarah.

"What is this for?"

"Just because."

"Hmm. Sounds like a reason you made up."

"Because you are you."

"Oh." Her eyes widened and a smile tugged at the curve of her mouth.

He snuck a look to the left and right, made sure no one was watching them and gave her a quick kiss.

The ride home was peaceful.

Noah had the driver drop Sarah off first, walked her to the door, kissed her again.

He was in the back of the car alone, headed to his home, when he allowed his thoughts to drift back to Gus. How many men and women like him lived in this area? What could he do to help them? And was he willing to step into the limelight to do so? Because he understood that the minute he started helping people who were addicted to drugs or alcohol, someone would start digging into his past.

And they wouldn't have to dig very far.

It was no longer a question of whether it would hurt his parents, or affect his relationship with Sarah. He was confident in both of those things.

The question was whether he had the courage to take such a step. Because once he did, there would be no turning back.

Chapter Thirteen

Three weeks later, Noah was walking to the parking area, walking hand in hand with Sarah, when a police cruiser pulled up beside him and stopped. Officer Hank Rodriguez stepped out. Noah had met him when he'd first returned home. As a condition of his parole, he was to check in with the local police department, and he had done so. He hadn't spoken with Rodriguez or anyone at the police station since.

And although he'd done nothing wrong, his heart rate accelerated, his hands began to sweat and he froze like an animal sensing danger.

"Mr. Beiler." Rodriguez nodded at Sarah. "Miss."

They both said hello. At least Noah thought they did. His mind wasn't working right. He could barely make sense of what Rodriguez was saying. He heard *come in…today…drive yourself or...* Above and beyond all of that, his mind was screaming *this can't be happening.*

"Why do you want him to come to the station?"

Sarah's words brought the present moment into crystal-clear focus.

She sounded calm, measured, polite. She sounded like an anchor he could hold on to.

"He's done nothing wrong," she added.

"We just need to ask him some questions." Rodriguez was speaking to Sarah, but his eyes were on Noah.

And suddenly Noah was able to speak. He couldn't stand there and let Sarah be his only defender. He needed to advocate for himself.

"*Ya*. Okay. I'll drive myself, unless..." He turned to Sarah. Her *dat* had already left. They'd stayed late working on the remodel for the market's front entry. They'd stayed late because they liked being with each other and neither wanted to go their separate ways.

"You could take my buggy to your home, and I'll... I'll pick it up later."

"*Nein*. We'll go to the police station together." She gripped his hand more firmly.

Rodriguez nodded once. "I'll meet you there, then."

He drove behind them, as if Noah might make a break for it in a buggy being pulled by a horse. As if Noah would be foolish enough to run. Running never worked. He'd tried it on his first two arrests. It only made him look guilty, and it was exhausting. That kind of fleeing, it was filled with anxiety and fear. He wouldn't regress to the person he'd been then.

"Any idea what he wants?"

"None." Misery had settled over him like a dark cloud. He'd never be free of his past. He'd never step out of that shadow. How had he allowed himself to believe that he could enjoy a fresh start? How had he dared to bring a woman into this mess that was his life?

"You've done nothing wrong."

"Innocent men go to jail, Sarah."

"You're not going to jail." She crossed her arms and glowered out at the summer day that was melting into night. "They can't do this. It isn't right."

Noah noticed every buggy they passed. Every person standing outside a business who looked up. Neighbors. Coworkers. Church members. All watching him drive slowly to the police station with a police cruiser shadowing him the whole way. The entire town would know his history now. Or worse, they'd make up one entirely based on their imagination.

When he pulled into the police station, he'd worked himself into such a state of despair that he wasn't sure he could set the brake, open the door and walk into the station. Sarah scooted closer on the seat, took his hand in hers and said, "Look at me, Noah."

He finally did. Tears stinging his eyes, his hands shaking, his heart quaking, he looked at her.

"You did nothing wrong, and you have nothing to be embarrassed about."

"But the Amish grapevine," he croaked. He pulled his hand from hers, covered his face, tried to still the fear building in his heart.

"Forget about that. It doesn't matter what people know or think they know. Look at me, Noah."

He finally dropped his hands and did as she asked.

"I'm going in with you. I'm going to wait in the lobby. They have a lobby, right?"

He nodded through his misery.

"Okay. I'll wait. And if they do decide they're going to keep you, I'll call my *dat*. I'll call Bishop Ezekiel. We're not going to let you spend even one night in jail. You've done nothing wrong."

Her confidence should have stilled his fear.

It didn't.

He'd been through this before. He'd been guilty then, and he wasn't now, but he had been through this before. The questioning. The arrest. The humiliation. And finally—resignation, because he couldn't fight the system. He didn't know how, and he didn't have the energy for it.

Five minutes later he was sitting in an interview room. This one was nicer than the one in Chicago. New carpet on the floor. Fresh paint on the walls. The two-way mirror was the same, though. The camera in the corner of the room blinked its light just as that other one had. The sense of being trapped was familiar and sickening.

The Shipshewana police chief was a woman. "I'm Chief Stillwell. You know Officer Rodriguez."

Noah nodded.

"I want to be clear that you are not being arrested. We simply want to ask you a few questions; however, you have the right to have an attorney present."

He stared at her.

"Would you like to have an attorney present, Mr. Beiler?"

"Nein." He cleared his throat. "No need for that."

"All right." She opened a folder sitting on the table between them. "According to our records, you were sentenced to ten years in the Illinois State Prison for possession and distribution of Schedule II drugs. Is that correct?"

Noah was staring down at the mugshot of him. He'd never seen it before. The man in the photo looked tired, ill, defeated. The man in the photo was without hope, and Noah remembered being that man. It was someone he never wanted to be again. He closed his eyes, pictured Sarah, his parents, his job.

"Is that correct, Mr. Beiler?"

"Ya." He opened his eyes, met her gaze, nodded.

"And you were paroled in April of this year."

"Correct."

She shuffled through the papers. "According to your parole officer, you've been working at the Amish market here in Shipshewana and you've adjusted well."

"I think so. That is to say, yes. I have."

She closed the folder and waited for him to say something else. But he didn't know what to say. He didn't understand why he was here. He had no idea what she wanted him to tell her. So, he did something that the Amish life had taught him to be very good at—he waited.

Finally she flicked her gaze to Rodriguez, who shrugged.

Clearing her throat and tapping the folder, she asked, "Do you know why we brought you in today, Mr. Beiler?"

"*Nein.* I have no idea."

"Someone's been selling drugs—Schedule II drugs—to our high school students. Adderall, Ritalin, hydrocodone, and Oxy. Do you know anything about that?"

"I do not."

"Have you been in the possession of drugs since your return home?"

"I have not."

"Have you facilitated the selling of illegal substances to minors?"

"No."

"Do you have any first-hand knowledge of anyone who has sold illegal substances to minors in Shipshewana?"

"No."

She waited a beat, then waved a hand to Rodriguez, who took up the questioning.

"We've kept an eye on you, Noah. I hope it's okay for me to call you Noah." He waited for Noah to nod. "It's part of our job. Nothing personal. Just trying to keep the community safe."

"Okay."

"As far as I can tell, you've kept your nose down. You go to work, go home, take your girl out now and then."

"*Ya*. That's about it."

"Tell us about your trip to Grand Rapids."

Noah's mind tried to digest what Rodriguez was saying. They knew about his trip to Grand Rapids? They knew he was dating Sarah? They'd watched him to *keep the community safe*. Did they honestly believe he was a danger to his neighbors and coworkers? To the children in both Amish and *Englisch* schools?

"Grand Rapids?" Rodriguez asked again.

"Amos—Mr. Yoder—sent me."

"Your boss?"

"Right. There was a conference of sorts on outdoor markets. He wanted me to go—me and Sarah. Attend sessions. Bring back ideas for expanding the market. I received approval from my parole officer. You can call him. His name is Tanner Pike. I can give you his number."

"We've already spoken with Mr. Pike." Rodriguez's voice was calm, and he looked directly at Noah when he asked his next question. "Did you go to Grand Rapids to procure drugs?"

"No!" Noah's temper threatened to spike, but he forced it down. "Look, I don't know why you're questioning me or why you're singling me out—"

"We're bringing in all parolees who were convicted of drug-trafficking charges."

"Okay. That makes sense. But I'm clean." He again closed his eyes, pulled in a deep breath, pictured the farm, his home, Sarah. Opening his eyes, he sat up straighter. "I'll submit to a drug test if you'd like. I haven't touched the stuff since that day over eight years ago when I was arrested."

Neither Chief Stillwell nor Officer Rodriguez responded to that.

"Drugs ruined my life. No. That's not entirely true. I ruined my life. I made terrible decisions. But I'm not that man anymore. Search my buggy. Search my home and barn. Ask my boss or my work crew or my girlfriend. Ask my bishop. I'm clean, and I have taken a vow to remain that way for the rest of my life."

Chief Stillwell allowed a whisper of a smile to cross her face. "Officer Rodriguez said the same thing."

"You did?"

Rodriguez shrugged, smiled, nodded.

"But we had to ask, Noah. We have to do our job." Chief Stillwell allowed something of the burden she carried flicker into her expression. "My first priority is keeping our teens safe. I will find who's selling to them, and when I do, I will press for the harshest sentence possible."

It was Noah's turn to nod.

In the deepest parts of his heart, he agreed with her. He agreed that strict sentencing was fair and just. He agreed that people who sold drugs to anyone—children or adults—deserved to be incarcerated. He had deserved to be incarcerated.

But those same people also deserved a second chance after they'd paid their debt.

Something passed between Chief Stillwell and Officer Rodriguez. It felt to Noah as if the tension had gone out of the air. Or maybe it was the threat that had evaporated away.

Was it over?

Were they going to let him leave?

Walking in, he'd imagined the handcuffs being slapped on his wrists. He'd heard the clang of the jail cell door closing, the key turning in the lock, the quick and sure death of all his dreams.

Chief Stillwell stood and offered her hand, which he shook.

"Thank you for coming in, Mr. Beiler. I admire your dedication to turning your life around." She hooked her thumbs into her utility belt that held her weapon, flashlight, handcuffs. "Any chance you'd be willing to speak with our students on Drug Day?"

"About what?"

"About your experience. It could go a long way to deterring them from ever getting involved with drugs."

"Umm…"

"Just think about it. Officer Rodriguez will see you out."

When Noah stepped into the waiting room, when he saw Sarah and realized that he was free to go, he thought his knees would buckle.

"Let's get out of here," she whispered and held his hand as they walked out the door, into the summer evening, and toward the buggy.

He stepped outside, stepped into the life that he had made, the second chance he'd been blessed with, and he very nearly broke down.

How had he taken it for granted?

And what was he going to do now?

"Let's go to the park," Sarah whispered.

"Ya?"

"Please. We need…we need a minute." She was grateful when he nodded. They needed time to recover, and she wanted to speak with him privately, before they had to answer any questions from their families.

He drove down the road, pulled into the parking area, directed Beauty to the back corner where they wouldn't be disturbed. From where they were sitting, Sarah could see children darting about on the playground, a young family enjoying a picnic next to the small pond, an old couple walking along the path.

She was ready to admit that she wanted that.

She wanted all of that.

She wanted her children to dash through a summer evening laughing and playing. She wanted to bring her family here for a picnic. She wanted them to one day be that old couple walking along the path. She was ready to admit that she longed for those things. And somehow by admitting those truths to herself, she found the courage to help Noah through this most difficult of days.

"Let's walk." She didn't wait for an answer. Instead, she hopped out of the buggy, gave Beauty a peppermint and waited for Noah to join her.

He sat there looking through the front window of the buggy, and the pain and worry and relief on his face nearly broke her heart. Noah Beiler was a *gut* man who had made some very costly mistakes. But that was behind him now. She only had to remind him of that.

Finally, he opened the door, got out of the buggy and walked slowly toward her. She slipped her hand in his, and they walked down the same path that the old couple had disappeared down only a few moments earlier.

The sun slanted through the leaves of the trees.

The children continued to shout and run and laugh.

The family having a picnic were now tossing a fishing line into the pond.

She glanced over at Noah. "Life goes on, *ya*?"

"Does it?"

"It does." She squeezed his hand and waited.

"I was so afraid, Sarah. More than the first time."

"Explain that to me."

"The first time I was arrested, in Illinois, I was arrogant. I knew I'd only get a slap on the wrist. It had happened to most of my friends. Correction, they weren't my friends. They were just other doomed individuals traveling the same path."

"And the second time?"

"The second time was worse. I was a little afraid. Most states have a three-strike policy. That should have been a wake-up call, but I was still using and the drugs gave me a strange kind of bravado." He chuckled, but there was no joy in it. "I thought I was a superhero."

"But then you were arrested again."

"Yup. The third time I was terrified. I knew that I'd crossed a line that there was no returning from. I was put behind bars, and I knew that I wouldn't be coming out for a very long time."

"Today must have brought up some very painful memories."

"Things I've been trying to forget. Even after sharing with your family, sharing with you, I refused to allow my mind to actually go back over the details of those days. The monotony of each one being the same. The frustration of being locked inside except for our one hour a day in the rec area—"

He laughed and that sound nearly broke her heart.

It had no humor in it. Only despair.

"It was basically a grassless area with a basketball hoop at one end and some picnic tables at the other. I'd walk the perimeter like a caged animal. I had this intense desire to stroll through a field or sit on a park bench or throw a fishing line."

Could he move forward? Some days she was certain that he had and he would. Other days, it felt as if they were sliding back to where they'd been months before.

"I've spent so much time trying to forget those years, but you can't forget the details—the horror of your past. They're like scars that you carry with you each day, that you see each day. You have to come to terms with them."

Sarah squeezed his hand. Walking seemed to be helping. Some color had come back into his complexion, and the fear that had crept into his voice was gone.

"Tell me what they wanted."

He went through the questioning and Chief Stillwell's explanation for bringing him in. He pulled her over to a bench and waited for her to look at him. "There's no use running from my past. It's part of who I am."

"I agree, but you haven't been running. You told my family. You speak with me openly about it."

"Ya." He stared off into the distance. "Being called in like that could happen again."

"Okay. Fine. We won't be as terrified next time."

Her words seemed to snap Noah's attention back to her. He touched her face. "You're pretty special. I guess you know that."

"I know that I love you."

"And I love you, Sarah." He pulled her into his arms and held her, held on to her.

Sarah knew then that they would find a way to adjust to this new reality. What option did they have?

As they walked back toward the buggy, Noah said, "Everyone will know now—everyone we work with, everyone we worship with, everyone."

"They'll know that you went into the police station, but it isn't as if your past will have been published in the paper."

"Their imagination could be worse than the truth."

"It could, but Noah…we can't spend the rest of our lives worried about what other people are imagining."

"You're right."

They'd walked slowly over to where they had parked. Instead of opening the door for her, Noah rested his back against the buggy, and Sarah did the same.

"It might be better to get in front of the Amish grapevine," he said.

"Do you have any idea how to go about handling the gossip?"

"Yes. I do have an idea."

She thought about that. She didn't know exactly what he had in mind, but she knew that she was ready. She felt as if her love for Noah emboldened her, made her strong, equipped her to face anyone and anything.

It would seem that they were about to find out if that was true.

Chapter Fourteen

The Sunday service that week was held at the Schwartz farm.

Sarah somehow made it through the sermons, which had seemed to take twice as long as usual. She tried to sing with the others, though she found herself forgetting the words to hymns she'd sang all her life. She earnestly prayed that *Gotte* would give Noah strength and peace and the words to melt hearts.

Finally it was time for him to address the congregation.

It was time for him to make his confession.

As she sat listening to Noah lay out his missteps, wrong turns and sins in front of their church, she thought that her heart had never hurt so much before. What he was doing took such courage that it was a wonder he was able to stand. She'd never been more proud of him.

Her *schweschdern* sat next to her—Becca, Eunice, Bethany and Ada. They sat as they so often did—oldest to youngest. Lydia rested on Bethany's lap, already fast asleep. Mary sat burrowed against Becca, sucking her thumb and playing with her *mamm*'s *kapp* strings. Rachel Beiler sat at the end of their row.

Across the aisle, her father sat with Gideon, Ethan, Aaron and Reuben Beiler. She thought her *dat* was one of the wisest, kindest men she'd ever known. She also thought Noah was very much like her father.

Noah had told her he thought it would be easier to share his past with the congregation now since he had already shared it with her family. *"I'll have my own support group out there among the larger congregation."*

"You most certainly will."

"I'm going to need it." He'd pulled her into his arms when he'd said that.

"*You don't have to do this*," she'd whispered.

"I know."

Watching him stand at the front of their congregation and recount his struggles as a young man, his addiction to drugs, his time in prison… it all made her love him more. The things he'd been through amazed her. What he'd endured. How he'd grown. That he was such a kind and hardworking man.

"Those years were terrible," he said now. "They were terrible because of what I endured, but more than that, because I came to understand what I had put my parents through. Over the months and years, I saw how I'd turned my back on all I'd been taught. I'd rejected a *gut* life and an all-encompassing faith. And now, in front of each of you, I vow to be faithful to my family, my friends and my Lord."

Sarah glanced down the row and then across the aisle. Her family and Noah's family sat with smiles on their faces. A few of the women had tears running down their cheeks. Even her own *dat* and Noah's *dat* swiped at their eyes. Ada was nodding and Gideon was grinning and Sarah understood that they all held tremendous respect in their hearts for this man that she loved.

"*Danki* for listening to my confession." Noah allowed his gaze to drift to Sarah. She gave him a thumbs-up, and his worried expression lightened. "If anyone has questions, please do come and ask me. If you have concerns, I want to hear them. Please keep me and my family in your prayers as we walk this journey back to the life that *Gotte* first intended for me."

Bishop Ezekiel stepped forward and placed a hand on Noah's back. Sarah hadn't realized how much the bishop had aged. His hair was thinning, his beard was now as white as snow and his skin as wrinkled as a well-used map. He used his cane more than ever, owing to the left knee he'd injured years ago. But he was the same Ezekiel. The same compassionate, wise man that she'd known all her life.

"In the New Testament, the book of Matthew, Christ tells the Pharisees that the greatest commandment is to love God, and the second is to love your neighbor as yourself. Mark records the same. And Paul, in Galatians, says that the entire law can be summed up in a single command—love your neighbor as yourself. It's plain what we are to do, *ya*?"

There were several *amens* and many in the congregation nodded in agreement.

"I have known about Noah's journey and his troubles since he was a *youngie*. I sat with Reuben and Rachel through many a dark night. And I was there with them on that glorious day when they welcomed their son home. As your bishop, it was my great pleasure to do these things. To see this young man come back into the fold." Ezekiel held up his Bible, presented the word to them. "Love your neighbor as yourself. Let us go forth and do that."

They stood to sing a final hymn, "Victory in Jesus," then the service was over. Sarah's family swarmed Noah and his parents. She remembered their discussion of bees, back when they were getting to know one another. A hive wasn't so different from a family, and they would protect one another. They would be there for one another, help one another.

Rachel pulled her into a hug, then they were both wiping tears from their faces.

"No more secrets," Rachel said.

"No more secrets."

It did her heart good to see her family supporting Noah. To see how much they accepted him—mistakes and all. She managed to get close enough to squeeze his arm. He whispered, *"Danki."*

Why was he thanking her?

All she'd done was fall in love.

As she helped in the serving line, she noticed a few of the church members seek him out. She could tell they were asking him questions. He would nod thoughtfully, lean forward slightly to listen better and finally respond. She hoped that they were being kind.

Twenty minutes later they were all seated—her large family of eleven with his family of three—squished together on the benches of three picnic tables that had been pulled together.

"No use beating around the apple tree," Ada said.

Noah leaned toward Sarah and asked in a mock-whisper, "Beating around the bush?"

"*Ya.* I think so."

Ada continued as if they hadn't spoken. "Folks were surprised by your confession, Noah. But I saw a lot of compassion and love in their faces. It's amazing how you were able to turn your life around."

"Didn't do it on my own." He nodded toward

his parents, who smiled. "Couldn't have done it without my folks supporting me."

"Well, I think you're the cat's purr."

"Cat's meow," both Bethany and Becca said at once.

Everyone laughed. Ada looked at Sarah and winked, and Sarah let go of all the tension from the last few days. She couldn't guarantee that everyone would be compassionate and loving, but the people at this table would be. That was what mattered.

It was later, while they were walking toward the Schwartz's barn to have a look at the new foal, that Sarah shared the idea she'd been chewing on since they'd left the police station.

"I've been thinking about what Chief Stillwell asked you to do."

"Speak to the *youngies*?"

"Right. And I think that would be a *gut* idea—speaking to Amish and *Englisch* teens. Think of the difference you could make. Think of how *Gotte* could use your journey to guide theirs."

"If I can face a hundred Amish as I confess my past, I can face an auditorium full of *Englisch* teens." He leaned closer and whispered, "I've heard Amish are quite conservative and old-fashioned in their ways."

"I've heard the same," she laughed.

He said more seriously, "Some in our community think that because we're plain, we're immune to drugs or alcohol or teen pregnancy. But it's not true. We deal with the same problems everyone else does."

"Ethan and Aaron dealt with some of that. There were a few who blamed their family situation on a lack of faith. Some felt that if their family's faith had been stronger, their *dat* wouldn't have suffered with bipolar disorder."

"But it's a medical condition."

"Exactly."

Noah sighed. "We have to accept the challenges we face if we hope to overcome them."

"Which circles right back to my idea. I was thinking maybe you could do more than just talk to *youngies*."

They'd reached the pasture fence next to the barn. She could just make out the foal with a star on its forehead, grazing next to the mare that had birthed it the week before. The colt's legs were impossibly long compared to its body. It jumped to the side, then scampered back, causing both Sarah and Noah to laugh.

New life.

The goodness of *Gotte*.

Everyday joys that always amazed her.

"Tell me more," Noah said.

"Maybe you could start like...well, like an Alcoholics Anonymous meeting, only for people who have struggled with drug addiction."

"Hmm. The *Englisch* actually already have that. It's called Nar-Anon."

"Okay. So we create a group like that. It would be open to Amish and *Englisch*. It would be open to their families. Your parents, they might be able to help other parents who are going through something similar."

"A support group."

"Exactly."

He didn't answer right away. Instead, he crossed his arms on the top rung of the fence and studied the scene in front of him. To Sarah it was quintessentially Amish—the barn, the horses, the field. The scene was quiet and peaceful. Simple. A reflection of their lives as well as their priorities.

Which didn't mean their lives were perfect.

Or that their priorities were always as they should be.

Every family dealt with missteps and heartache.

And Noah was right—some within their community denied that such problems even existed.

"I think you could help. I think that maybe *Gotte* brought you back here for that reason."

He turned and studied her, and then he pulled her into his arms. "I have never in all my days met anyone like you, Sarah Yoder. You're one of a kind. Did you know that?"

"I am?" She pulled back so that she could look up at him properly.

"You are."

"I was thinking the same about you."

He caught her hand in his and they turned to walk along the fence line. "Tell me how this idea of yours would work."

They tossed around thoughts about where the meetings could be held, how often they would take place and what they could do to get the word out. They began a mental list of who might be interested in helping. As a solid plan began to form, Sarah knew that Noah had done the right thing by sharing the details of his past. Now the question was how people would receive it. They had no control over that.

Instead, they would leave the results in *Gotte*'s hands.

They would step out in faith.

The first support group meeting was held at the coffee shop next to JoJo's Pretzels on a Saturday morning. Two moms showed up. One was Amish. The other *Englisch*. They were next-door neighbors, had watched their sons grow up together, had watched both young men descend into a world that was inconceivable to them.

"We couldn't believe it was happening."

"We didn't know what to do."

"But we could see they were hurting."

"Hurting and unable to ask for help."

Noah was immensely glad that Sarah was there

with him. Mostly they listened to the heartache and worry and dread that these women carried. When they were talked out, when they seemed spent from unburdening themselves, Noah offered suggestions for ways they could be supportive but still firm. Sarah promised to pray for both young men and reminded the ladies to return for the next meeting.

"Hopefully we will be able to support one another," Sarah said.

"Hopefully we can begin dealing with these issues instead of sweeping them under the rug," the Amish woman said.

Her friend nodded in agreement, then added, "It's so good to be able to talk to someone about the things that weigh on our hearts."

"Thank you for doing this, Noah."

"Couldn't have been easy."

"You can be sure we'll be back for the next meeting."

For the second meeting, Noah's parents came along. They also had the same two moms from the first meeting, plus a father and three teens. For thirty minutes, Noah told his story and answered questions. Then his *mamm* chatted with the two moms, Noah and his *dat* spoke with the father, and Sarah spoke with the teens.

As the group was breaking up, Noah was surprised to look up and see Officer Rodriguez standing at the back of the room. This time his hands didn't sweat and his heart rate didn't soar. He didn't know why the officer was there, but he knew that the man wasn't there to arrest him. Noah introduced Sarah and his parents. The officer shook hands all around. He wasn't wearing his uniform—just jeans and a T-shirt. Just a guy in town who happened to stop by the coffee shop.

It could have been a coincidence.

Or not.

"I heard about your group," Rodriguez admitted. "I have to say, I'm impressed."

"Why?"

"Because it would be easy to try and hide from your past, Noah. That's what most people do."

"Doesn't work."

"I agree." He allowed his gaze to travel the room, pass over the people who were gathering up their things and leaving, offering Noah and Sarah a small wave, looking a bit lighter for what they'd shared. Officer Rodriguez added, "Not everyone will appreciate that you're doing this."

"What do you mean?"

But Sarah was smiling and nodding her head. "I heard a woman in the back complaining. It was while you were sharing, Noah, so you might not have noticed her."

"What did she complain about?"

"That kids these days thought everything could be solved by talking it out. That a firm hand was what was needed. She only stayed a few minutes, then went out the door muttering about consequences."

"She's not wrong about either of those things, but consequences can be balanced with love and compassion. That she couldn't see that...well, there will always be naysayers."

Noah's *mamm* tsked, and his *dat* patted her arm.

"It's better to hold out a helping hand than to point a finger," his *dat* added, then he grinned when Officer Rodriguez looked stumped. "Amish proverb."

They all walked out together into a day that was spitting rain. But Noah knew that even rain was a blessing. His life was so full, so satisfying, that he wondered how he had ever doubted it could be so. A small part of him was afraid that he'd take a wrong step and lose it all. A bigger part of him knew that wasn't going to happen. He would make missteps—surely, he would. But they wouldn't be of the drug variety. And he wouldn't lose his family, his community, or Sarah.

For the third meeting, they had to push several tables together. Over a dozen folks were there, plus Noah, his parents, and Sarah. The question-and-answer period took much longer, but it was a good time of sharing. Not only did the group promise to meet again the following week, several had friends or family that they hoped to bring.

"We might need a bigger meeting space," Sarah said as they drove home.

"I'm still surprised to see the *youngies*. Takes a lot of courage for them to come to a meeting like that."

"I didn't hear what they said to you afterward. Had all three used drugs? Or is that private information?"

He reached over and squeezed her hand. "Two had experimented and were worried that they were getting in over their heads. We're going to have an accountability group that meets on Tuesday afternoons every week."

"That's great!"

"I think so. The other was a teenage girl worried about her older *bruder*. He left home a few months ago, and they haven't heard from him since. Apparently his *dat* caught him using and issued an ultimatum, which is understandable. But it's also why he left."

"What a sad situation."

"It is, but it's also pretty normal, and that's what I told her. We'll pray, and we'll try to help her family be ready for when he comes home again. Most people do, eventually, return home."

Though it had been raining, the August day was hot, and Noah suddenly had a hankering for something cold. When he pulled into Kukui's Hawaiian Shaved Ice, Sarah looked at him in surprise.

"What?" he asked.

"We just left the coffee place."

"True, but I didn't eat a thing and I'm pretty sure you didn't either."

"*Ya*, who had time to eat? We were busy making people feel comfortable."

"Exactly. Time for a treat."

Sarah ordered a rainbow ice, and he opted for pineapple.

They were sitting at a little table with small metal chairs. Sarah's lips were stained red from the cherry flavor in her shaved ice. Suddenly, at eleven-thirty on a Saturday morning in late August, Noah realized with crystal clarity how much Sarah meant to him.

He understood that he wanted her in his life forever.

He still didn't know exactly how his future would unfold. Who did? But he knew that regardless of the details, he wanted to spend it with the woman now at his side.

The only question that remained was what he was going to do about it. Sarah was special. She deserved a well-thought-out plan. He would do this carefully and prayerfully. He'd take his time, and he'd do it right.

Chapter Fifteen

The last Friday in August was also Sarah's last day to work on Noah's renovation crew. The next morning, she woke determined to keep busy and not dwell on things that might or might not be happening at the market. She swept, mopped, dusted. Cleaned, scoured, bleached. Finally, she could think of nothing else to tidy, so she decided to work on her dinner prep—outside.

"Aren't you going to miss it?" Eunice asked.

They were sitting on the front porch. Sarah was snapping green beans. Eunice was working on a gadget that Sarah couldn't identify.

"Where did you get that?"

"Zeb gave it to me."

"Zeb?" Sarah couldn't stop the smile spreading on her face. "Zebedee Mast? I didn't know you two were—"

"We're not. And you can stop smiling."

"Doesn't he have a little boy? His wife died of cancer, right?"

"*Ya*. It's all terribly sad, and Zeb is still very much grieving."

"I guess it takes time."

"No doubt. He moved back into town a few weeks ago."

"And you're not interested?"

"In being a stepmom for a man who is still grieving his late wife? No, thank you."

"Okay."

"Not everyone in this family has to be married or dating."

"Got it." Sarah held up her hands. "Sorry I pushed. It's just that I worry about you."

Eunice rolled her eyes. "Zeb heard I had a knack with mechanical things and challenged me to fix this piece off an old water pump."

"Looks pretty rusted up."

"The first of many problems with it. But we were talking about you. Quitting your job? Trading the busy days at the market for life on the farm?"

"Right. Well, I'll miss spending my days with Deborah and Andrew and Stanley. They're going to miss the market as much as I am."

"Noah's whole crew is quitting?"

Sarah laughed. "Now you sound like him. But it's not exactly true. Deborah is going to help out her *schweschder* who lives in Lancaster."

"For how long?"

"As long as she needs to. Her *schweschder* is

having twins, and she already has four children, so…"

"Yikes."

"Yup. She hopes to return in a few months, but who really knows?"

"And the guys?"

"Stanley promised his parents he would try one semester in college. On a whim he applied to one of the midsize colleges in Texas—Texas State, I think—and they accepted him."

"Which leaves Andrew."

"Right. Andrew will be helping his *dat* with the harvest and then the fall planting. He hopes to return when those things are done, and if he has it his way, he'll sign on permanently. The work really suits him." She snapped a few more green beans. "Say, how would you like to work on Noah's crew?"

"Nope."

"That was a rather speedy response."

"Because I don't need to think about it. I'm the only Yoder girl who hasn't worked at the market, and I'd like to keep it that way."

"You've helped every year at the Christmas market."

"Yup."

"Sounds as if you know what you do and don't want."

"Yup."

Sarah tossed what she hoped was a motherly look at Eunice, who only laughed and said, "Okay. You explained why everyone on Noah's crew is quitting, but you haven't explained why you quit."

Sarah's hands stilled over the bowl of beans. "I like working at the market, but it's not what I want my life's work to be."

"You've thought of your life's work?"

Sarah laughed. "Cooking, cleaning, caring for my family…those are the things that I'm very *gut* at. And yes, it helps to take a break and do something different for a time."

"Like work on a seasonal crew."

"Right. But I'm more comfortable here. I like being on the farm. With Ada, Becca and Bethany expecting…"

"It's seriously crazy to think we will have five babies in the family by this time next year."

Sarah nodded. She could see it. She could envision their ever-expanding family gathered in the sitting room or around the table or out under the maple trees. But in those visions, she had started seeing herself beside Noah with a child of their own, and now she didn't know if that was going to happen or not.

"Some serious thinking going on over there."

"Indeed."

"Let me guess. You thought Noah would ask by now."

Sarah's head jerked up.

Eunice merely shrugged. "Not that hard to figure out, sis. It's plain as the beans in that bowl that you're in love with him."

"I won't bother denying it."

"And he loves you. I know he does."

"He's said as much."

"But still no marriage proposal. I do not understand men."

"Who does?" Becca laughed when they both looked up in surprise. "Didn't hear me walk up, did ya? If I was a snake, I could have bit you. Both of you were quite preoccupied."

"It's not like you arrived to the clatter of horse hooves."

"Nope, I walked."

"All the way?"

"All the way."

They all looked over at Becca and Gideon's house. It was positioned two dozen yards from the main house, and it seemed to Sarah that it had always been there. That it belonged there.

"Where's Mary?" Sarah asked. "We definitely would have heard you if Mary was with you. Your darling little girl is a chatterbox."

"She's with Gideon. That little sweetheart is a daddy's girl. No doubt about it."

"And soon she will have a *schweschder* or *bruder*."

"Maybe you'll have five." Eunice laughed. "What? I don't mean all at once, and five is a *gut* number. There were five of us and look how well things turned out."

Becca sank onto the porch step and rested her back against its post. "Slow down, sister. One *boppli* at a time, please."

"Unless you have twins," Sarah pointed out.

"Unless you have twins," Eunice echoed.

"Do we even have twins in our family?" Becca rested her hand on her stomach, which hadn't yet begun to show evidence of her pregnancy. "Feels like one to me. Now back to what you two were talking about."

"What was that?" Sarah resumed snapping green beans. She was thinking about how *gut* it felt to sit here in the late summer sun with two of her *schweschdern.* At the same time, her dreams were tap-tap-tapping on her heart, reminding her how much she missed Noah.

Eunice explained about Sarah's last day at work and that they were both wondering why Noah hadn't proposed.

"Maybe he's scared."

Sarah's hands stilled over the bowl of beans. "Scared? Scared of what?"

"I can think of a lot of things." Becca began to tick them off on her fingers. "Scared he won't be able to provide for you and a family in the way that he'd like to be able to. Scared he's not *gut* enough for you. Scared to ask *Dat.* Scared you don't feel the same. Scared he'll backslide into drugs. Scared—"

"Stop right there." Sarah set the bowl of beans on the floor next to her rocker and stretched her back. "You're wrong about the last two."

Becca cocked her head.

Eunice stopped working on the water pump.

"He knows I love him. We expressed our feelings to each other weeks ago. And he knows he won't backslide. He said nothing could ever tempt him back into a prison cell again."

"Back up a minute." Becca dropped the hand she'd been using to tick off Noah's possible fears. "You said you loved him?"

"Ya."

"And he said he loved you?"

"*Ya*. He did."

"Then what are you worried about? Give the guy some time."

"Except she's not getting any younger," Eunice said.

"Ouch. That was like an arrow to the bull's-eye."

"She is thirty-one," Becca said.

"Also, I'm right here. I can hear you both."

"There's one scenario we haven't considered." Becca leaned forward to mock-whisper to Eunice. "Noah could be asking *Dat* this very minute. Or he could be sitting in his little office, writing down how he plans to pop the question."

Sarah suddenly couldn't sit there a second longer. Her patience was about to snap like one of the green beans in her bowl. "You know what. I think that I have a kitchen sink to scrub. So if you'll excuse me..."

"Don't be that way," Becca said, her voice suddenly gentle and sweet. "We were only teasing."

Eunice nodded in agreement. "We'll stop if you'll stay."

Sarah had reached the door. Now she turned and smiled at them. "I don't mind the teasing, but honestly, I don't know why he hasn't asked yet. I can't think of a single solid reason for him to hesitate. And I refuse to be the kind of woman who sits around waiting for a man to make up his mind."

Becca's and Eunice's eyes went wide in disbelief.

She supposed she had sounded rather radical—for an Amish woman anyway. But she was a modern Amish woman. She didn't need a man to complete her or to give her purpose in life. But, oh, how she did love Noah Beiler.

She went inside and scrubbed the sink.

Then pulled the kitchen rug outside and beat it.

Then tossed together a chicken, green bean and potato casserole and put it in the refrigerator until it was time to bake it.

And all the while she was working, she was thinking that there was one person who might know what was on Noah's mind, what was in his heart. Other than Noah, of course. She wasn't quite ready to quiz him about his intentions. But perhaps it was time to make a move of her own. She went to the barn, harnessed Oreo, their oldest mare, to the buggy, and called out to Eunice that she'd be back in an hour.

It was time to find out just where, exactly, she stood with Noah. She wanted to know. She deserved to know, and besides, as Eunice had pointed out, she wasn't getting any younger.

Noah was late getting home, owing to the fact that he'd stayed to interview people for his work crew. He still couldn't believe that Amos had turned his position into something that was both full-time and permanent. The man's confidence in him was something that he was grateful for every morning.

He'd told his *mamm* that he would probably be late and not to hold dinner for him. When he arrived home, it was seven in the evening.

"I'll take care of the mare, son." His *dat* winked. "Your *mamm* has your dinner in the oven."

In fact, his *mamm* was sitting at the table, working on some type of knitting. He never could figure out what she was making until she'd finished it, and then it was so obviously a sock or a sweater or a baby's jumper that he felt foolish for not recognizing it.

"Your food's in the oven."

"*Danki*. I'll just wash up first."

By the time he joined her at the table, his stomach was rumbling, and he practically inhaled the food.

She waited until he'd poured a second cup of coffee from the pot on the stove—after confirming it was decaf—and then she patted the seat next to her. "Sit back down. I want to talk to you."

"Uh-oh."

She laughed, but when she set aside her knitting, he knew she had something serious to say. "Sarah came by to see me today."

"She did?" He couldn't think of any reason that Sarah would visit his *mamm*, but then again he never claimed to understand women. Maybe she had stopped over for a knitting lesson.

"I like her."

"*Ya*, I do too."

"But how *much* do you like her?"

He'd been reaching for an oatmeal cookie, but his *mamm*'s question stopped him in his tracks. "I love her, *Mamm*. I've told her I love her. She knows that. Was she asking if I loved her?"

"Don't get all worked up."

"Okay." He picked up two cookies instead of one, then set them down beside his coffee cup. Suddenly, he didn't feel so hungry. Sarah had stopped by to see his *mamm*? And the two of them had talked about their relationship? What did that mean? "What's this about?"

She reached for his hands, patted them, then stood and refreshed her own coffee. Finally, she sat back down. "What Sarah said to me, she said in private. I won't betray that confidence."

"But you brought this subject up for a reason."

"I did."

"And the reason is..."

"To remind you that there is a time for everything."

"Huh?"

"A time to be born. A time to embrace. A time to love."

"Yikes. Amish proverb?"

"Ecclesiastes. Old Testament." She relaxed back in her chair, rotated her cup left, then right. Tossed him an apologetic smile. "I'm not doing this very well. To tell you the truth, I had sort of put these hopes and dreams away, tucked them into a box and told myself not to think about them."

"Dreams? What dreams? Are we talking about you now or are we still talking about Sarah?"

"Noah." She waited until he quieted, until he was completely still and paying attention. "I want to be a *grossmammi*. Your father wants to hold his *grandkinner*. I'm not saying that to pressure you in any way. Your life is just that—your life.

But I feel the need to share with you that we love Sarah, and you've admitted that you do too. So, what are you waiting for?"

He was stunned.

"Take your time," she said gently.

"Well..." He gulped the coffee and immediately regretted it. His stomach was unsettled enough. "Well. I just recently found out I'm employed full-time."

"True."

"I wanted to be sure I had a steady job."

"Understandable."

Noah felt sweat trickle down his neck. He knew his *mamm* wasn't pressuring him. She was helping him face the big questions, but he'd already been facing them every night as he tossed and turned. There were so many questions, so many details, and each time he thought he'd answered one, he had to backtrack and assess the previous one again. The result was that he ended up more confused than when he started, and he was also pretty tired the next day. He'd taken to telling himself to think about it later, out of pure self-preservation.

His *mamm* was still waiting.

He pushed the coffee cup away. "I need to work out where we would live. This house isn't very big. Plus, there's the fact that her family depends on her. It could be that Sarah would rather live there."

He hesitated, fell quiet as the questions swirled in his brain. What would be the first step? How did one go about this? "I want to talk to Amos first, get his blessing. I know it's not necessary, but it seems like the right thing to do."

"For a minute, let's forget all of those things."

"What? How can I—"

"Forget all of that, Noah. Forget where you're supposed to live or what your job will be or how her family will respond. Those are details. Those are things that you and Sarah, and Sarah's family, and me and your *dat* will all work out. They're just…details."

"Okay."

"You love her."

"I do."

"And she loves you."

"*Ya*. She does. Sarah's great. She's more than I could ever have dreamed of in a *fraa*. She's kind, patient, understanding. She makes me feel as if anything is possible. She makes me feel whole again. I don't want to mess this up, *mamm*."

"Do you really think you could?"

"Mess it up?" He stared at the ceiling. "You're talking to a guy who spent eight years in a state prison."

"We're not talking about that. We're talking about you and Sarah."

"Right." He crossed his arms, then uncrossed them. "Right."

"Do you honestly think there's any way you could mess up your relationship with her?"

"*Nein*. I care about her too much, and she cares about me too much for that. We're solid."

"That's *wunderbaar* to hear."

A silence filled the room, and instead of it making Noah more nervous, he felt calm. The questions that had been circling in his mind for so long finally stopped spinning. His fears stopped spinning.

"So, you're saying…" He gulped. "You're saying that I should ask her?"

"You should ask her."

"Is that what she said?"

"Private conversation."

"Oh."

His *mamm* stood, rinsed out her mug and kissed his cheek—making him feel five years old again. Also making him feel loved and cared for and accepted. He sat there at the kitchen table for a long time. Heard his *dat* come into the house. Heard his parents' voices as they softly spoke to each other. Heard them say good night.

He stayed where he was.

And gathered his courage.

Because his *mamm* was right.

It was time.

It was time to ask Sarah to be his bride.

Chapter Sixteen

The next day their church congregation met for worship at the bishop's house. Sarah gave Noah a small wave as she and her *schweschdern* took seats on the women's side, one row up from his. She never again looked his way. She seemed completely focused on the singing and the sermons, as she should be. As he should be. But Noah's mind kept replaying what his *mamm* had said.

Those are details.

You should ask her.

There is a time for everything.

All his life, it had seemed that Bishop Ezekiel managed to somehow touch on what he was personally going through. It seemed that the bishop, in his wisdom, knew and then planned his sermon or his scripture reading accordingly. So, Noah shouldn't have been surprised when one of the Bible chapters Ezekiel quoted from was Ecclesiastes, chapter 3. "There is a time for everything, and a season for every activity under the heavens."

Noah sneaked a peek at his *mamm*, who was

sitting with the Yoder *schweschdern*. She glanced back at him, smiled, then turned her attention once again toward the bishop.

Noah had tossed for hours the night before, thinking about what his *mamm* had said, wondering what the true reason was for his hesitation. He thought it was that he didn't believe he deserved someone like Sarah. However, he'd lived long enough and made enough mistakes to know that love wasn't something you deserved. It was something given.

If Sarah loved him, which he knew she did…

And if he loved Sarah, which he knew he did…

It was only his fear standing in the way.

He knew what he wanted to do, what he needed to do. And he'd waited long enough.

He managed to have a word with Becca first by waiting outside Ezekiel's house. She'd gone in to rock baby Mary, who was teething and a bit cranky. Becca stepped out into the late summer sunshine, then jumped when Noah stood from one of the rockers.

"Gave me a fright, Noah. I didn't see you there."

"I was wondering if we could talk for a minute."

"Of course."

Becca was able to tell Noah that Sarah's favorite color was yellow. "Not bright yellow. A soft, buttery yellow. But why do you need to know that?"

"Something I'm planning."

"Okay. Whatever it is, I'm sure she'll be pleased."

"Don't mention anything to her."

"Of course not." Then she'd patted his arm and hurried off to find Gideon.

Bethany was certain that Sarah's favorite food was pizza, which reminded him of their first lunch together. "You're sure?"

"Positive. As many toppings as possible. But no anchovies. She hates those and always picks them off."

Pizza and the color yellow. Two questions answered.

When he asked Eunice if Sarah had a favorite spot in town, Eunice started laughing.

"What's so funny?"

"You've already been there with her—the barn quilts. And if you're looking for a private place, there's a nice picnic area across from the Schwartz barn, and yes—they have a quilt square painted on that side."

"Thanks, Eunice."

"You're welcome, Noah." Then she promised to keep it between them.

Barn quilt, pizza and the color yellow.

He went in search of Ada. "Morning, afternoon or evening?"

"Sarah's always been partial to a walk in the afternoon." She threw her arms around him before he could say another word. "I won't spill the yarn."

"Spill the beans?"

"Don't know about that, but I've knocked over a yarn basket before, and those balls roll all over the place. It's a real mess to clean up." Then she, too, patted his arm and hurried away.

Afternoon, barn quilt, pizza and the color yellow.

He might not know the details of their future, but he was determined to give her the perfect proposal. Sarah deserved that. Which meant he had to go and talk to Amos.

There was absolutely no reason for him to be intimidated by the man. Amos Yoder was a fine boss and a friendly person. He was someone who Noah had come to respect and trust. He would be happy to have the man as his father-in-law.

Father-in-law.

Was he really going to do this?

Yes. He was. As he walked over to where Amos was standing at a pasture fence, watching sheep, he felt as if his throat was so dry he wouldn't be able to speak a word.

"Noah, *gut* to see you. Fine Sunday, *ya*?"

"It is." And those were the only two words that came out. He tried to swallow. Tried to slow the beating of his heart. Tried to calm himself. This was supposed to be the easy part. This was merely a formality.

But what if it wasn't?

What if Amos wanted more than an ex-con for his oldest *doschder*?

"Something you'd like to say, Noah?"

"*Ya.*" He gulped. Wished fervently for a glass of water.

"Take your time, son."

And it was that last word that gave him the courage to plunge forward.

"I love your *doschder*, Amos. I love Sarah, and I'd like to marry her. That is, I'd like to ask her to marry me. But I want, *nein*, I need your blessing. I'm probably not the kind of man you envisioned for your *doschder*, and I know that you're taking a risk with me, but I also believe that we've developed a *gut* relationship. You know I'm a hard worker. You know that I'm determined not to slip back onto the dark road I traveled before. And I promise you, Amos, I promise that I will love and treasure and care for her and for our children, should *Gotte* bless us with any." He sputtered to a stop.

"Finished?"

"*Ya*. I think so."

Amos had been watching him closely through the whole speech. Now he reached out and put both hands on Noah's shoulders. He waited until Noah met his gaze. "You are everything I could have hoped and prayed for in a son-in-law. Sarah, if she says yes, will have a faithful friend, a *gut* husband and a *wunderbaar* father for her children."

"Seriously?"

"Yes. Seriously." Then Amos pulled him into a hug.

Noah was at first embarrassed that there were tears in his eyes, but then he looked at Amos and saw that his eyes were shiny with unshed tears too.

"Welcome to the family."

"If she says yes."

"Oh, right. When are you asking?"

"Tomorrow. I'm going to ask her tomorrow."

"She's standing right over there, Noah." Amos nodded toward his family, who were oohing and aahing over a new puppy.

Sarah might have sensed that they were watching her. She glanced up, looked at Noah, her father and then again at Noah. Finally, she offered a small wave.

"You could have your answer in the next few moments."

"*Nein.* I want to do this right. I… I have a plan."

"I see."

He did go over to Sarah, though. He managed to ask her if he could take her out tomorrow afternoon, if he could take her to dinner.

She looked surprised, but she said yes.

She said yes.

And he took strength from that. Once back at

his house, he asked his *mamm* what he could use for a picnic blanket. He was shocked when she pulled out an old quilt made of the softest squares of yellow. "This was your *grossmammi*'s quilt. Your *dat* and I used it for picnics when we were courting."

He somehow managed to sleep that night.

And he arrived at work at sunrise the next day so he could leave early.

Everything except the pizza was in the back of the buggy—the quilt, a quart jar of sweet tea, some of his *mamm*'s oatmeal squares, napkins, glasses. He placed the items in the picnic basket that he'd found in the barn. He'd brushed the dust off, placed all of the items inside, set the entire thing on top of the quilt, and prayed that she would say yes.

He would pick up the pizza after he picked up Sarah.

She was waiting for him on the front porch—looking fresh and relaxed and hopeful. Was he imagining the hopeful part?

They spoke of the market, what projects she'd begun working on at home, the upcoming fall festival. The conversation helped to relax him so that at least he stopped sweating. When he pulled up to the pizza place's drive-thru window, she laughed.

"What?"

"You seem to have this all planned out."

"*Ya*. I mean, you like pizza, right?"

"I love pizza. Everything except—"

"Anchovies." They both smiled, as if he'd discovered a big secret.

When he directed Beauty into the picnic area across from the Schwartz farm, Sarah hopped out of the buggy quickly, gazing across the small county road. "That's one of my favorite barn quilts. We didn't get to see it when we were on our barn quilt date."

"Seems like just yesterday." He walked up behind her, put his arms around her.

"It does, doesn't it?"

He wanted to ask her then, but he realized that if things went well, this was a story that they would tell their children and grandchildren. There was no need to rush things.

He laid out the yellow quilt. Sarah took off her shoes, then sat on it, running her fingers over the small blocks of fabric. "This is lovely."

"*Ya*? My *mamm* said her and *dat* used it for picnics when they were courting."

"It's hard to imagine our parents courting."

He knew then that Sarah was thinking about her father, about the fact that he would be alone if she married and Eunice married, though as far as he knew Eunice wasn't even dating. Also, Noah didn't think Amos would ever truly be alone. He had a solid family, one that would always enjoy and seek out his company.

They ate pizza, basked in the last of the sunshiny day, spoke of small things like childhood memories and favorite books and what they enjoyed most about the change of seasons. Noah realized that he wanted to know everything about this woman beside him, and even though they'd worked together all summer, even though they'd spent many days together, there was still much he didn't know.

And suddenly he couldn't wait another moment.

"Marry me."

"What?" Eyes wide, a blush creeping into her cheeks, she asked, "What did you just say?"

"I asked you to marry me. I love you, Sarah Yoder. I want to spend my life with you." He pushed the pizza box out of the way and reached for her hands. "Do you love me?"

"I do."

"Will you marry me?"

Her smile was all the answer he needed, but it was still *wunderbaar* to hear her say, "I will."

He wanted to stand up and shout it to any passing car. He wanted to put it on the marquee outside the Blue Gate Theater. He wanted to tell the world that Sarah had agreed to be his bride.

"I was hoping you would ask soon," she admitted.

"Seriously?"

"*Ya*. We're not getting any younger."

"Eh...we're not that old."

"Old enough, Noah Beiler. If we want to have children, we need to get started soon." Then she slapped her hand over her mouth, as if she'd suddenly realized what she'd just said.

Noah wasn't embarrassed.

He started laughing, and then she joined him.

Finally, she clarified, "Thirty-one might not sound old to a man. But for a woman, well, if we want children..."

"If *Gotte* wills it, then we will have children, Sarah. And if not, then we will find other ways to fill our home. The important thing is that we'll be together."

He jumped to his feet, paced toward the buggy and back again as the worry and tension of the last few days left him. "We're getting married."

Sarah stood, walked to him, walked into his arms, and planted a soft kiss on his lips.

It was a scene that he couldn't have imagined ten years earlier, or six months earlier, or two weeks ago. He'd known that he loved her for some time now. But he'd recently come to understand that their love was mutual and it was strong. It would be enough to sustain them.

He stood there with the bright blue Indiana sky above them, the barn quilt in the distance, the yellow quilt a few feet away, and Sarah Yoder in his arms. He was the happiest man in Shipshewana, in all of Indiana.

Maybe in all the world.

As they drove home, they discussed their hopes for the future. How many children they wanted. Where they would live. What their families' reactions would be. How soon the bishop would approve their marriage.

"I have a feeling he'll waive the six-month period that he usually recommends for couples." Noah smiled and reached again for Sarah's hand. He felt complete when she was next to him. He felt as if he could face the world—the past, the present and the future.

"We'll still have marriage classes to attend."

"I'm looking forward to it."

"Really?"

"Sure. There's no telling what I'll learn about you."

"Yikes."

He laughed, and then she joined him.

Noah understood in that moment that his life was a miracle. *Gotte* had taken his mistakes, taken his detours and wrong turns, and used them all to lead him to the woman sitting beside him, the community around him, the life that exceeded his wildest dreams.

He could hardly wait to see what was next.

It was the fourth wedding in three years for the Yoder family. Sarah thought she shouldn't be nervous, that she should be experienced enough to be an *Englisch* wedding planner, or at least an Amish one.

"But this is your wedding, Sarah." Becca adjusted her *schweschder*'s new apron, then smiled at their images in the mirror. "That makes it different."

"That makes it special," Bethany agreed, reaching for baby Lydia before the child had a chance to snag the small bouquet of flowers that Sarah would hold.

They didn't go all *Englisch* with the wedding plans, but they did celebrate with the things they loved. The caterer would serve a traditional meal. Bishop Ezekiel would preside over the wedding. And the arch they would stand under would be adorned with white and yellow roses.

Sarah loved roses. Loved the smell of them, the sight of them and the soft color of them.

Her *dat* had ordered buckets full from the local florist. "My oldest *doschder* is marrying," he'd said. "There's no order of roses that would be too large for this celebration."

Ada sighed wistfully. "I remember when Ethan and I tied my *kapp* strings."

"Tied the knot," Eunice laughed.

They all laughed.

"Oh, it's a bucketful of laughs now, but just wait until I need a new dress." Ada touched her stomach, which was just beginning to show signs of her pregnancy. "Come to think of it, new dresses are a *wunderbaar* part of expecting."

"Speaking of expecting… I believe the bishop is expecting Sarah downstairs."

Each of her *schweschdern* kissed her on the cheek as they filed out of the room.

Becca said, "*Danki* for always being there for us."

"I am so excited for you two." Bethany pressed her cheek against Sarah's. "It's thrilling to see the way our family is growing."

Ada dabbed at her eyes. "I'm going to smear my makeup."

"You don't wear makeup."

"*Ya*, but if I did…" And then Ada threw her arms around Sarah and hugged her tightly. "Thank you for being like a mother to me."

There had been a time when Sarah felt weighted down by the responsibility of caring for her family, when she'd worried she didn't have what it took to be a *mamm*.

But they'd learned together.

They'd learned to be a family.

She looked out of her bedroom window, saw their friends and family gathered there under the maple tree that was shedding leaves of red and brown and gold. The October day had dawned sunny, warm, perfect. She missed her mother terribly in that moment. She supposed that she'd never stop missing her. But she also felt overwhelmingly grateful for her *schweschdern*, her brothers-in-law, her *dat*. It seemed to her that *Gotte* had stitched together a beautiful tapestry in spite of their loss. He had looked at that eleven-year-old girl, mourning her mother, and even then he had a plan for her.

Sarah walked down the stairs, to the sitting room, to where her soon-to-be husband waited next to Ezekiel. Together they talked and prayed, read from the book of Corinthians, and then prayed some more.

She could hear the first of the hymns being sung. It was one of her *mamm*'s favorites—"I Will Sing of the Mercies of the Lord." And wasn't that a testament to her life and Noah's life and the life they would share?

Ezekiel reached for their hands, clasped them in his. "Not every day will be this beautiful, this happy, this perfect. But you will always have the memory of this day to help you through the more difficult times. You will always have the love of your heavenly Father, the support of your family and your commitment to one another. And it will be enough."

Together they walked out into a fall day so beautiful it caused an ache in her heart.

Noah waited patiently until she looked up at him. "Ready?"

"*Ya*. I am."

He reached for her hand, laced his fingers with hers and together they stepped into their future.

Epilogue

Sarah and Noah stood on the banks of Lake Michigan.

One thousand miles of freshwater coastline.

Actual beaches and beach towns and trails through the dunes. The day before they'd visited a local lighthouse. It was all amazing and special. They were making memories that she would treasure the rest of her life. This man beside her she would treasure the rest of her life.

"You're right," Sarah said. "The lake is bigger and grander than I imagined."

They were staying in a cottage up the road, enjoying a proper honeymoon. Noah had confessed to her that it all seemed a bit extravagant, though more and more young Amish couples were taking a few days away. It wasn't as if they flew to Hawaii, but it still felt like a very special gift. One her *dat* had insisted on paying for.

Noah reached for her hand. "Are you sure that you feel okay moving in with my parents?"

"I do. They missed you terribly when you were away, Noah. I don't want them to be alone again."

"Yes, but your *dat*..."

"Has Eunice there with him, plus Becca and Gideon and Lydia."

"And soon a new *boppli*."

"He won't have a chance to be lonely."

"Do you think he'll date someone? Now that you're married?"

"There's still Eunice in the house, remember."

"True."

"Though I'm wondering if she might have her eye on a certain young widower in our congregation."

"Zeb Mast?"

"Maybe. She denies it, but she also blushes whenever his name comes up."

"Ah, young love."

"As for *Dat*, I haven't noticed anyone that he has taken a special interest in." She sighed and clasped Noah's hand as they walked along the shore of the Great Lake. "I will have to trust that *Gotte* has a plan for my father."

"He had a plan for us that I would never have imagined. Remember that first night I came to dinner? You pretty much apologized for your *dat*'s match-making attempts."

"We didn't know if *Dat* was trying to match you with me or with Eunice."

"Seriously?"

"*Ya*. I remember her coming into the kitchen and saying *I think this one's for you*."

"Wow."

"I know!"

"Guess I owe Amos a great big thank you because it seems like he knew what he was doing after all."

They walked for another half hour, then turned back toward their cottage. Sarah loved being away from the farm, being alone with Noah for a few days, being able to rest and simply enjoy each other's company. But she was also looking forward to going back to Shipshe and setting up their little room in his parents' home. She was looking forward to getting to know Rachel and Reuben better.

It seemed to her that life was blossoming into something wondrous, and she was ready to embrace every change, every challenge and every joy the coming days would bring.

* * * * *

Dear Reader,

Sometimes our past can get in the way of our present.

Sarah Yoder has a history of running away from romantic relationships. It's not because she's flighty or immature. It's because she's convinced her family needs her. She's certain that now isn't the time to embrace her own dreams. Then Noah Beiler walks into her life.

Noah has a past that he's ashamed of and secrets that he's determined to keep. But relationships are stronger than secrets, and Noah's past is just that—in his past. It takes courage, as well as the faith of both him and Sarah and their love for each other to see their future and to be willing to embrace it.

I hope you enjoyed reading *The Mysterious Amish Bachelor*. I welcome comments and letters at vannettachapman@gmail.com.

May we continue "giving thanks always for all things unto God the Father in the name of our Lord Jesus Christ" (Ephesians 5:20).

Blessings,
Vannetta